ARTIFICIAL SNOW

FLORIAN ZELLER

ARTIFICIAL SNOW

Translated from the French
by Sue Rose

PUSHKIN PRESS
LONDON

English translation © Sue Rose

First published in French as
Neiges artificielles © Flammarion 2002

This edition first published in 2008 by
Pushkin Press
12 Chester Terrace
London N1 4ND

ISBN 978 1 901285 84 0

Cover: *Annual Rings* 1968
© Dennis Oppenheim
Courtesy of the Artist

Frontispiece: Florian Zeller 2006
© Arnaud Février Flammarion

Set in 11 on 13.5 Monotype Baskerville
and printed in Great Britain
by TJ International Ltd Padstow Cornwall

Ouvrage publié avec le concours du
Ministère Français chargé de la culture—Centre national du Livre

Where goes the white when melts the snow?

Attributed to William Shakespeare

Soon it will be Christmas. Yesterday, at two in the morning, I returned to the avenue where I live, my childhood avenue, the one I'd watched so many times from my window, late at night, in the run-up to Christmas, waiting for it to divulge its secrets. In the frosty moonlight, the pavement was white as snow. It seemed that from up there, my forehead still pressed against the glass, the boy I used to be was watching this traitor return.

Jean-René Huguenin

Boring Prologue

I really thought I was done for. Until then, death had never been a particularly daunting destination. It was a future, perhaps, something quite abstract that can't really be imagined, because it's still a long way off, over there, just ahead. Myself, I felt immortal.

When I was a kid, I used to travel a lot. I'd shut my eyes and off I went. I was particularly fascinated by the universe, the planets, stuff like that. I wanted to be an explorer when I grew up. All the countries had already been discovered, the only thing left was the mystery of stars and comets. And words.

I travelled through space. I was looking for the frontier dividing the universe from the rest. I thought matter couldn't possibly be infinite and I spent hours trying to visualise that boundary. Who knows, these might have been the early signs of a raging neurosis.

Death caused me pretty much the same problems as the concept of infinity: I found it absolutely impossible to *see* what it meant. I once had a dog that was found run over three streets from my house. That was pretty much all I knew about it.

But one day in November, the day she left me, it was my heart that was found run over and life really began to get boring. I'd just realised it was all a big con.

So I set about trying to find an idea that I wanted to live and die for, some kind of justification, a *raison d'être*. Needless to say, I drew a blank, consigning my dreams of adventure, grand destinies and magnificent things to the gutter. Because nothing, absolutely nothing, denied my absurd and ludicrous existence.

I struggled for several months. I really thought I was done for. Everything seemed terribly boring: getting up in the morning, going to bed at night, pretending not to pretend, shaking hands, being polite and romantic, studying and getting good marks, everything. I even found the prologue of the novel I was trying to write after a fashion tragically boring. But, then again, deleting it was even more boring. That's probably how I began writing.

When it came to boredom, I had a reliable point of reference: Adam. He must have been bored to death too in that apple-filled garden of his. Naturally I'd read the weighty tome telling how woman had been created, how divine mercy had wangled man a reprieve from boredom, if only for ten minutes a day, twenty for the most talented studs, and I'd realised that boredom was at the root of demography: the greater the boredom, the bigger the population. Put another way, everything pointed to one obvious deduction: the world had never been so boring. Especially China.

Then, a few weeks ago, I had a hunch, a strange thought, and I came to the conclusion that it's not worth spending too much time trying to work out the meaning of the world, its possible logic, its probable failure. Going down that road was bound to lead to a dead end, a cold, forbidding emptiness.

I'd drunk quite a lot that evening and, in a sudden moment of clarity, I understood what Bacon was getting at when he suggested that things are actually quite simple: we're born one day and we die another, and that's all there is to it. If anything happens in between, so much the better.

That's how I look at things now; with a feverish determination to fill that interval waiting to exist, cram it full of everything that stays, everything that isn't yet dead. And forever find a road a little less empty, a little more infinite, in a love that's renewed nightly.

I'd like to answer the world's absurdity with its beauty.

Its beauty is commensurate with everlasting wonder.

PART ONE

Chapter One

Every end does not appear together with its beginning.
Herodotus

1

I'D DRUNK FAR TOO MUCH to accept the idea of being deserted again, but no two ways about it, there was no one left on the platform. Fuck! I'd just missed the last metro.

That's how the story begins. And why not? You can have some incredible adventures just because you've missed a metro. It seems like a pretty plausible beginning to me.

To be honest, it wasn't an isolated case. In the past week alone, I'd missed about ten metros. And always in the most exasperating way: I'd hear the doors-closing alarm echoing through the corridors and, just as I hurtled onto the platform, gasping for breath, I'd see the metro slowly pulling out, as if nothing were wrong.

The recurrence of these incidents seemed to give them a mystical significance. Along the lines: everybody's gone, except you; or: you're the only one waiting for a train that's just gone, again.

The word 'train', when I spelt out the problem, was enough to make me feel depressed. I thought, not unpoetically, about the trains you wait for that never arrive. But poetry didn't solve everything because, in my case, the metro had arrived and had even stopped for a while. It was just that the sodding train had pissed off without waiting for me.

I started wondering what this constant stream of near misses was telling me, whether there wasn't, behind the banal everyday details, a meaning, a message. If this wasn't a roundabout way of showing the world that I was one of life's inveterate losers.

2

The way things are, everybody, at some point in their life, feels a complete failure; for me, that point had joyously started the day I was born and seemed dead set on continuing indefinitely. That's why I sometimes experienced trivial events, whether bound up with the metro or not, as a central collapse of the soul.

Depression sees everything as evidence of despair. At that point in the story, I wasn't completely up or completely down. I was on my knees trying to resist the temptation of salon nihilism or fashionable disenchantment, which would have been so easy. Not that I was enchanted really. I was somewhere in between, uncertain.

Enthusiasm was the only antidote to uncertainty I'd found. I sometimes discovered relics of hope embedded in me like fossils in ancient stone, an odd collection of elements that everything seemed to repudiate. I foresaw glimpses of a magnificent future that made the listlessness of my current existence even more unbearable and I set out again with these encouraging glimpses in the torn pockets of my memory. I puffed out my chest and, shaking my fist, repeated a phrase I've never really understood, but one that, I was sure, showed a certain understanding of human nature: *after me, the deluge*.

But this time, I said it silently. Nothing came out of my mouth. After me, nothing. Before me: nada. Without me: exactly the same. If it came to the crunch: *without her, the deluge*; anyway, I'll say more about that later.

3

Watching the metro pull out of sight, I realised very matter-of-factly that life was completely getting away from me. Certain strange phenomena, like missing metros, were a daily occurrence, but their root causes remained obscure. In my heart of hearts, I wasn't desperate to understand them. Man only survives life by regularly eschewing the next level of comprehension.

And yet I was unsettled. I was trying hard not to confuse leaving things to chance with that worrying premonition of the unknown. Life seemed riddled with signs, codes and coincidences. Several times I'd passed a face virtually identical to mine in the street. The idea that I might not be unique after all was pretty unpleasant. The thought that I was just a number, just one more face, the repetition of a perpetual visual zero was downright disagreeable. This experience called to mind the story of an explorer who'd discovered an unknown, lifeless body preserved in the ice at the heart of the North Pole. Edging nearer, he'd been seized by unspeakable terror when on closer inspection he realised that the ice was a mirror and that he could see *himself*, on the other side, held captive for many years: the same face, exactly. He'd just found his own father, who had disappeared years before on an expedition. They were both thirty-one, in that strange world formed of ice and oblivion, father and son, exactly the same face. They looked each other straight in the eye; they could even have pinched each other if the ice had not come between them.

4

I felt like that explorer, except for the cold. Something meaningful was taking place before my very eyes. The platform was empty.

Obviously, none of it meant anything specific; you couldn't add impressions like numbers to form an equation; there were no answers and the question itself wasn't terribly clear. It was just disconcerting. I'd said to myself at the time that I ought to make a note of that story of the explorer somewhere, so that I could use it in a future novel, were I ever stupid enough to start writing. Because, with a little luck, the rest might be contaminated by its enigmatic subtlety.

It appears that Nietzsche's present success can be explained in part by the development of public transport. It's certainly true that the notion of a power conflict becomes pretty tangible when we sweat in public, when we're being smothered by coats, bags, the interminable faces of others, and when, at rush hour, everybody discovers they have all the skills of a killer as a fold-down seat finally comes free.

Unfortunately for me, that evening, I wasn't meant to have this nihilistic, deeply philosophical experience, because—and this is the point I was trying to make— I'd just missed the last metro.

Chapter Two

Today, nothing.
Louis XVI

1

I RETRACED MY STEPS BACK to the same chilly
passageway with the uncomfortable feeling that
I'd failed. As if the experience I'd just had, although
banal, wasn't entirely mine, as if I'd totally lost control of the stubborn, unruly moment. I sometimes felt
like a stranger to myself, as if I were letting myself
float on some calm, relaxing, unknown sea. I regularly forgot the features of my own face, then recalled
them as one might remember a trivial detail, a remote
fact frustrating the urge to forget. At times like this, I
was surprised to be the person I was and not someone else. Was I an individual? I think I can say that
I felt things individually—pleasure, disgust, anxi-
ety—I even sometimes used first-person pronouns
with a transitory feeling of humanity, but I still can't
say whether *I* really belonged to me; so I kept looking
and continued to put on a show of individuality, until
I found whatever it was. In any case, one thing was
sure, I was going to have to find a taxi if I wanted to
get there.

2

I was supposed to be meeting the others in half-an-hour. People had been talking about the Star for months, but I'd never had the chance to go. I'd been told that the door policy was extremely selective. The idea of selectiveness was crucial for clubs like that. Luckily Florian had managed to lay his hands on some invitations for us. On the face of it, we had nothing to lose.

I couldn't tell you why I was so fascinated by that place. To be honest, I can't even say that I'd had a premonition about what would happen that evening. I'd been waiting for this party for days, like a childhood Christmas, as if I hoped it might save me in some way, but I couldn't work out why. Anyway, my phone was the latest Sony, in platinum, with every option under the sun. I liked holding it in my hand because it was particularly light. It shared a basic characteristic of everyday life: unpredictability. Anything could still happen. Everything could still be saved.

I could hear my feet echoing in the metro passageway, I felt like singing or shouting, but I didn't, convinced I was being watched. I never felt completely free from some sort of presence, an annoying, imaginary presence. This meant I was often extremely sociable. That evening, for instance, I could've killed two blokes. The first because he'd spilt his drink over my shoes, the second because he started laughing like a moron. I hated morons.

I have to point out that I was on my way back from a dinner party awash with them. Florian had told me it was better not to turn up at the Star before midnight and I'd said I'd go to this dinner party first. Marie had been inviting me regularly and I'd been cancelling at the last minute for over a month. My gut feeling hadn't let me down before that evening.

I hardly opened my mouth at the dinner party, except to eat. I was just waiting for the party later on. I didn't suspect that at the same time an incalculable number of metros were running, disgorging and devouring a formless mass of anonymous passengers, that everything was running *normally* and that this magnificent structure would collapse the minute I stepped onto the platform. I'd read several essays criticising the mechanisation of the world. Machines were taking up more and more room, they were gradually becoming indispensable in all walks of life. It was getting so that we didn't even notice them. We were forgetting how dependent we were on them. But I wasn't the type of person to criticise these changes. I even felt a certain indifference to tedious alarm-mongering talk. Yes, people lived by machines. Yes, people were losing their humanity. So what? So, nothing.

In my view, people who wallowed in nostalgia as they watched what was taking place before their very eyes hadn't by definition understood anything. Changes in the world have always been accompanied by a sense of decline. Always, in every day and age. There was nothing original about ours. The forces might be a little stronger, since there was the feeling that the current changes were far deeper, far more frightening,

23

but the principle remained the same, a simple process of evolution.

So we had arrived at a state of ultimate dependence. Dependence led to fragility and fragility to uncertainty. I sometimes wondered what would happen if the great machine installed to run our lives collapsed before our very eyes. Like everybody else, I'd heard about the probable failure of computer systems with the new millennium. That would have been a real nuisance for me. As it was, I struggled to change my vacuum cleaner bag when it was full and I knew very well that the human race didn't stand a chance if anyone was depending on me to act in the event of a general implosion.

In the end, we woke up on the first of January feeling relieved. Nothing had happened overnight. We'd just lost a few fanatics with exotic aspirations. Nothing serious when it came down to it. Life went on. But I couldn't help wondering what would happen if everything did break down; I really wondered what would be left of mankind. These were the sort of stupid ideas that often occupied my thoughts.

3

So I'd spent several hours bored to death at Marie's place. She'd ordered in sushi and plum brandy. As usual, I'd really struck lucky: I was sitting next to a fat pig.

I'd decided not to sit down first, because you never know *who* will take the seat next to you. The safest technique is to wait a little, pretending to be interested in a revolting photo in an imitation-silver-supermarket frame—oh! isn't that nice!—then sit down afterwards, when the first bums are on seats, regally choosing the pertest. Unfortunately, I'd failed dismally at this. Unable to find a photo that could justify a slight delay in the rush for empty chairs, I'd fallen back on a calendar that I'd miraculously found in the toilet and, in the time taken to peruse it, everyone had already sat down. The only free seat was next to Pig.

I'd hoped, stars twinkling in my eyes, that the unused cutlery on my left heralded the late arrival of a sleeping beauty just woken from her long slumber, but I'd forgotten that the light of the stars can also reach us a long time after they've died. Marie stood up and asked us all to move round one seat and I found myself wedged between Pig and a cold radiator. That was when she told us we were having sushi. I spent most of the dinner party watching the Palaeolithic phenomenon on my right, who was sitting with his thighs so wide apart that I was forced to twist round on my chair. One detail intrigued me: a thin thread of dribble continually linked his mouth to the Japanese chopsticks that he frequently plunged into the communal pool of soya. For some unknown reason, I soon lost my appetite and concentrated on the plum brandy.

Finally dessert arrived. According to my tipsy calculations, the dinner party would soon be over and I'd have enough time to catch the last metro. Suddenly the lights went out, a shock fit to startle any dozing guest. My immediate thought was that the great human machine had just ground to a halt! But no, some girl was already on her way back from the kitchen bearing candles cleverly arranged on a cake. Was she going to replace the fuses? No, she seemed to be heading towards the table instead. What exactly did she mean to do? It was when she placed the cake in front of Marie and a familiar-sounding song rang out in the apartment that I realised all this had something to do with a birthday. Basic logic, which I usually wielded with dexterity, led me to suppose it was Marie's birthday, since the cake had been placed right under her nose. I glanced furtively right and left, no one looked surprised, it was just me. Everyone had taken out gifts. I even heard her say she was really touched that nobody had forgotten.

So I made the most of a moment's collective in-attention to take refuge in the toilet, just for the sake of diplomacy. (Anyway, I wanted to check something in the calendar.) I let some time pass and, just before March, two girls plonked themselves right in front of the door, out of earshot of the living room, and—misery of miseries!—started discussing their love lives. This was probably going to take ages and I couldn't really see myself coming out of the toilet, looking innocent, when they'd already been standing by the door for five minutes. Even the technique of coming out whistling wouldn't work. I didn't stand a chance. I could always have left at a run, but was that really a solution? I was probably going to miss the last metro anyway.

Anyway, Marie was a nice girl. I remembered going out with her when we were teenagers. We'd met in hospital. A mate of mine had gone in for an operation and I'd visited him every evening after school. At first, it was just for moral support but things soon took a completely different turn. Marie also knew him and like me visited him in the afternoons. I thought she was very pretty. We began to see each other more and more, in that squalid hospital room, staying with our friend later and later, as if we felt increasingly responsible for his pain. Poor guy. Then again, we didn't want to tire him out by staying too long, so we soon started meeting in the hospital cafeteria. The day we kissed for the first time, on the bed next to his, we decided it was better to let him convalesce in peace in future. Especially as the creaking of the bed can't have helped his afternoon naps.

But our romance didn't last long. I'd been seeing her again for the past few months and had the vague feeling she was trying to get closer to me. It wasn't that I didn't like her, she was actually rather attractive, but something was stopping me. We'd spent a few nights together at the time and I didn't like the idea of doing something I'd already done before. I felt that repeating things was always proof of failure. Getting back together with a girl was like admitting you hadn't found anything better since, it was like admitting you'd reached your sexual peak somewhere between fifteen and sixteen; that sucked. Which was why each day was a unique opportunity for me to start over. All I was looking to do when I went out was bring back a girl I didn't know, break the vicious circle of repetition. The only thing that interested me on a night out was pulling new girls. Naturally, in times of need, I would sometimes bring back girls I'd already slept with, but that was largely because I was in dire straits. I knew there'd be plenty of beautiful girls at the Star.

As a result, when Marie contrived things so that we bumped into each other in the kitchen and undid the top of her dress revealing her two pale breasts, I looked the other way and affectionately rejected her. Deep down, I had a very good heart.

In the taxi, I was thinking of an Italian sentence. It came from *Don Giovanni*. The opera.

Purché porti la gonnella, voi sapete quel ché fà.

That meant: you know what he'll do with her if she wears a skirt. I'd noticed that words soon got spoilt and that this trend was aided and abetted by the same type of erosion as the one that eats away at desire. Every phrase we mechanically repeat over and over is empty. We say things and, by saying them, we cause them to die a death. Which is why, for instance, you shouldn't tell a girl you love her too often. Or why it's advisable to go to mass as little as possible.

Everything pointed to the fact that a dangerous epidemic had contaminated language; its symptom was an ongoing process that automatically brought what we said down to the level of empty, everyday phrases—so even that remark became inexcusably banal. I hated small talk and dinner-party conversations, I hated listening to people in the street. When it came down to it, people were strange characters. Total dickheads, even. The proof they were all dickheads was that everybody said so.

We finally reached the Saint-Germain district. The smell of leather in the taxi was making me feel sick. I could see fashionable boutiques through the window, all the trophies of high society, luxury and beauty. That day I had in fact just bought a linen suit from Armani. The sales assistant had been unbearably beautiful. I was even in two minds whether to kiss her in the changing rooms. Because, personally, I knew what I wanted to do with her, with all those skirts; I had plenty of ideas, but when it came down to it, I couldn't. That meant I sometimes dreamt about it. I'd been told that dreams help to consolidate information acquired during the day, which seemed particularly ridiculous given that you can very easily dream on days when nothing at all has happened. Still, it was quite surprising that the little waves sent to the visual cortex, those ponto-geniculo-occipital waves, should in my case automatically take the form of a particularly inviting naked woman. Somebody once told me it was an obsession.

7

Was I a sex maniac? To be perfectly honest, I think I might have been. Either that or my subconscious was sorely lacking in imagination. I could pretty much imagine what you were supposed to do when you fell in love with a girl (go hang yourself). But what did you do when you felt in the mood to love all women at the same time? I really didn't know and, as with all great uncertainties, it resulted in disaster, debauchery and desertion.

The way I functioned was actually very simple. I was only attracted to a girl so long as she resisted me: all that happens when a thought meets an obstacle is that passions are aroused rather than subdued. This equation for sexual pleasure is a constant feature of human nature, a given in people's psychological make-up: we want what we don't have. That's why love's a rip-off.

As far as I was concerned, streets and parks, any public place where I wasn't left to my own devices or my own feelings, were free spaces where I could freely turn predatory at the sight of a pretty girl. Apparently, there are insects that die the instant they're impregnated. I'd think about them, sometimes, when making love, since this was the way of all pleasure: the moment of supreme sexual enjoyment preceded death and disgust by a second, one solitary second.

The weather was particularly sultry that evening and I began to regret not wearing my linen trousers. The radio was talking about the Arab-Israeli conflicts and a former minister who'd been accused of forgery and using forgeries, and I wondered if my trousers would go with my new blue shirt, all the while realising I'd never asked myself this question before.

I stylishly tidied my hair with the aid of the window, and the mocking smile of the driver reappeared in the rearview mirror, giving me to understand that he thought I was a complete arse.

I changed position to reach for my packet of cigarettes, but the rearview mirror coldly indicated, by reflecting a finger pointing to a small sign, that there was no smoking in the taxi. Fine.

I would gladly have initiated some kind of conversation with the driver, since the situation invited it implicitly, indirectly, despite being fraught with an obvious embarrassment that was almost palpable from the look on my face and, as a result, particularly oppressive—but what could I say? The real question was largely my angle of attack, the remark that would allow me to do my job, fulfil my social duty to reach out to others, and keep them as close as possible; even if this meant not being true to myself, turning myself into a metaphor for a social puppet that had nothing in common with who I really was, who I thought I was, a puppet pretending to laugh at the enforced abdication of its strings, its movements, its identity.

So the remark, but what remark? There was always the weather, which involved a couple of risks to be ignored at my peril. First off, I probably wouldn't have been the first person that day to pull that one and I really didn't want to piss him off, because when a taxi driver's got it in for you, he drives more slowly on purpose, he brakes miles in advance so that he has to stop at every red light and may even go so far as to take a detour or two to make you cough up even more. The other risk, in complete contrast, had more to do with a situation in which, suddenly rescued from an oppressive silence, he might begin listing the entire weather forecast for the week and, as a result, drive just as slowly.

Starting a conversation is as hard as starting a novel. This comparison wasn't much help though; I couldn't really see myself coming out with: "I've been going to bed early for ages, but tonight I'm going to see some friends at the Star." Or: "I really thought I was done for, but instead I decided to meet up with a few mates in a trendy nightclub." Better to keep quiet. Which is what I was doing more and more anyway, keeping quiet. Because, for a little less than some time, I hadn't really been wanting to talk any more.

Without her, the deluge.

I looked at the dark sky through the window. You'd have thought it was mid-August, at night, when storms and rain hang in the air. When you sense it can't pretend to be summer forever.

8

Lou. That was her name. Things turned out very differently with her. An exception in my relationship to the world, a subtle discrepancy. I knew she'd be there and it wouldn't take much for me to admit that my real reason for wanting to go to the Star was to see her.

I don't think you can really say it was love and yet, in a way, I loved her. And in another way, I was madly in love with her.

But platonically.

I thought the idea of platonic passion was wonderful. OK, it's true she was encouraging me, since she was completely ignoring me. But still. When I was with her, I was a different person, I lied through inability. She had a casual presence that robbed me of myself; to cut a long story short, I didn't think about sex at all. Strangely enough, those were the times when I thought most highly of myself.

A month ago, she came back. In my dreams, she called me "my darling"; in reality, she didn't call me at all, despite the messages I left on her answer phone. The most saccharine music got to me, arousing a latent nostalgia in the silence. At night, I didn't sleep, or found it difficult; I'd lie there in the dark, eyes closed, inventing dangerous situations that would allow me to see her again, win her over again. That didn't stop me from looking at other girls or continuing to be a premier-league sex maniac. But, what can I say, I focused mainly on her.

We'd met several years before, we'd gone out for a few months, we'd lived part of our lives together, as close as can be, then she left me. Apart from the end, this relationship had been totally different from anything I'd experienced before and, in some ways, I still carried, like an injured dog, that rapture inside me. The break-up had been painful, but I'd got used to it, and I'd done everything I could to rally to the world's slogan, the one marketed by Baudelaire himself: *Intoxication is a number*. I'd been blind drunk for a little less than six months, then we'd bumped into each other by chance, the other day, at a dinner party given by a mutual friend and, since then, I'd been catapulted back into the past. My moral decline was beautiful, since it hadn't taken me away from her for too long; beautiful, because beauty is never what you head towards, but what you come back to.

My relationship with other people was intriguing in that I couldn't survive without one of their number now.

Charlotte had told me Lou would be coming to the Star. I'd put on a pair of black trousers I liked and a grey Lycra shirt. I'd also cleaned my ears with cotton buds. I was full of hope. You might say that, in some ways, I was as perceptive as Louis XVI when he noted in his diary on 14th July, 1789: *Today, nothing.*

Chapter Three

The mud is red or black.
Arthur Rimbaud

1

I'D RECEIVED THE INVITATION the evening before, it was in my pocket, or more precisely, it was in my hand which was in my pocket. I was keeping a firm grip on it for fear of stupidly mislaying it. From what was written on the card, the theme for the evening was *The Future of Man*. I thought again, heading towards the main doors, about the dust we were all destined to become, as if there were a weird loop linking origin and future. Picturing Courbet's pornographic paintings, I thought there was something rather attractive about this prediction.

The Future of Man. I didn't know whether you were supposed to wear fancy-dress or whether you had to refer to this theme in some way, so, not being sure, I'd bought a box of Bromazepam with the idea of attaching it to a string, putting it round my neck and possibly hanging myself with it. In the end, though, I decided I'd better not draw attention to myself. Anyway, outside the Star, I noticed that no one had the same view of the future. Some people had even risked furs, sequins and latex. The mood in the queue was more optimistic than anything else.

Then came the selection ordeal, because I knew it took more than an invitation to get into this establishment. And, in fact, the door was blocked by exactly the type of bloke, probably a bouncer, who seemed to prove Darwin's controversial theories single-handedly and who, despite that, didn't throw me out but checked my invitation and let me in. No two ways about it, we really were descended from the apes. The bouncer hadn't even come down from his perch, probably through vertigo.

A girl pulled back the red curtain and, the very moment I walked in, the thought hit me that this was actually the Star. I might bump into some celebrities, but the idea left me cold. I refused to give in to the extraordinary appropriation of history's puppets, which meant you had to be Caesar—or nobody. As far as I was concerned, there was no contest, I was a complete nobody.

The lighting was low and it was very crowded. I walked around to find Florian and the others. Because of that business with the metro, it had to be at least one in the morning, if not later. There were little candles on each table and you could barely see what was going on in the darkness. In my imagination, I could make out bodies touching, caressing, licking each other, even more if the chemistry was right but, actually, you couldn't see very much. The girls were in very short things; I slowed down in front of couples who were kissing or girls who were drinking brightly-coloured cocktails. There was one very tall brunette in particular who was kissing a well-dressed guy; they seemed to be in love. It was sickening.

I scanned the horizon of bodies and sweat, trying to catch sight of Florian, but to no avail. The dress code was actually very casual; the thought crossed my mind that I looked like a civil servant or the foreman of a cleaning crew. Let's face it: what on earth had possessed me to dig out this bow tie? That said, it was dark and no one gave a toss.

2

At last I caught sight of Florian. He was talking to some people in a corner. In the candlelight, some guy was caressing the breasts of a blonde who was looking straight at me and to whom I nodded hello. It was Jennifer, an American, hi, how do you do. Charlotte was also there, but she was on her own, no sign of Lou, do you know if she's coming? No idea, she just said she might. Florian looked odd. He was smiling so much that he seemed deeply unhappy. He shifted along a little to make room for me on the banquette.

"So what've you been up to? We've been waiting for you for hours."

"I missed the last metro," I replied mechanically, as if I'd prepared my answer in advance. (I had a great sense of repartee.)

"Did you take a taxi?"

"Yep."

Florian was a strange guy. He was twenty-one and a bit. Quite a bit. His life had been turned upside down by one incident and he'd never been the same again. When he was ten, during one of his experiments, he'd poked a piece of wire into an electric socket while holding it in his mouth. The experiment had been conclusive and the reaction instantaneous. He'd been hospitalised for several days, since the electrical discharge had lasted for almost a minute. It was feared he'd lose the power of speech but, after intensive care, the only after-effects were a fierce desire to write books and a weird hairstyle: his hair seemed to be permanently crystallised on his head like untidy stalagmites.

He poured me a drink without a word. We'd met at secondary school. I hadn't liked his hair, which he wore blond at the time, and we hated each other. He had a cold, forbidding expression, while I was constantly searching for friendship. In the summer, we both went on holiday to the same Brittany village, our two houses were only a couple of streets apart. We'd sometimes bump into each other, although we didn't speak, until the day we became virtually inseparable for no good reason. Our common enemy—because sharing enmity is the best way of cementing friendship—was the kids we called "the wimps", the ones who let themselves be boxed in and did nothing about it, the ones who sat back and did nothing as their childhood fires were extinguished; our common enemy was the people we'd become, sad cases who took everything a little too seriously.

But what else could I have become? There were great hopes, moments of brilliant joy, but the dust had gradually fallen back to earth; I sometimes felt I was on the verge of being dead to myself and, faced with this little death, I had no last words, no grand farewell, no new and original theme. I had the feeling I was going to die without saying anything much.

First, I'd fallen into the trap. I'd wanted to be famous, me too. I'd wrongly thought I was suffering more than other people, for the simple reason I could feel my own suffering and not that of others. And this superior suffering implied, I fancied, a splendid, chaotic destiny. But I spent more time inventing this destiny than building it; I was trapped by a hope that employed me part-time and often took the impossible form of demanding achievement. With the result that a little later, largely through cowardice, I'd abandoned these plans to fall back on small pleasures within easy reach. I'd finally decided to live a simple life without having anything to prove, except to the woman I loved. That would be enough.

3

The woman I loved.

I still didn't see her. I'd thought I'd recognised her several times, but as the woman drew closer, I realised her figure bore no resemblance to Lou's wonderful body. To judge by the staccato rhythm with which I was tapping my cigarette against the ashtray, I must have had a bad feeling. In my heart of hearts, I didn't really know what I was expecting of her. I'd been aware, when we'd seen each other again, of a coldness in her eyes that suggested she no longer loved me, that she might never love me again. But I was trying to play down this upsetting observation by reminding myself that she'd always been cold, distant and inaccessible. I remembered for instance the few times I'd seen her cry; she wept big tears, unusually big, and often I couldn't work out where they came from, what they meant. She said it was nothing, that she sometimes felt desperately sad and it was nothing to worry about. All I knew was that the bridges between us were suspended above an abyss of incomprehension and that the slightest wrong move could result in a fall.

"Have you had them before?"

"What?"

Florian and Charlotte were looking at me enquiringly.

"Have you had the cocktails at the Star before?"

"No, I don't think … "

"They're solid cocktails, made of jelly and alcohol."

"Jelly?"

"Mm, jelly, like American jello. It's like having pancakes with Grand Marnier, you get drunk while you're eating."

American like jello, Jennifer was standing in front of me, moving her body in time to the music. The effect was reminiscent of the jello in question. She took a few mouthfuls and held out her hands to get us to dance with her. "We're coming", said Florian, and Jennifer went back to the dance floor.

Florian stood up, I stayed on the banquette. I didn't like dancing, there was something spontaneous about it that wasn't really me. Charlotte was also there, we were both staring into space. I had the acknowledged advantage of having a glass in my hand, which gave me something of an air of assurance. Made me look a little less like an arse, anyway. I gazed into the distance to see what she was looking at; nothing special, it seemed. We had something in common.

I wondered what I was doing in a place like this and I thought about Lou. She was the only reason I was here after all. I couldn't relate to clubs; they made me feel trapped and claustrophobic. And, in broader terms, I couldn't relate to my time. It was as though I was moving through it without really connecting with it. Or, more precisely, I felt a kind of nostalgia for a life I hadn't lived, inexplicably wallowing in a sweet sorrow for an invented past or an uncertain future; and this feeling of disconnection was sometimes so strong that it felt like my life was no longer taking place in the present.

Carmen sat down opposite and we said hello vaguely; she was wearing a white dress that set off the sun-drenched colour of her skin. She had something about her, the way foreigners do; Florian had told me she was Spanish. Despite the music, you could make out her singsong accent from a long way off. She smiled black and blue. Black for her hair, blue for her infinite gaze. And to think that the girl had killed a man.

I remembered an anecdote about her that Florian had told me. Carmen had gone out with an older guy with a vast collection of works of art. He'd taken her somewhere for the weekend, say Normandy, and they'd made love for *two whole days*. On Monday morning, she'd found she was lying next to a corpse. According to the experts, he'd died in the middle of the night from a heart attack.

I didn't really know if the story was true or if, as so often is the case, it was full of dubious projections and imaginings, but that wasn't the issue. There's a word to describe the simultaneity of death and orgasm, 'epectasy'. I remembered I'd been particularly interested in that anecdote at the time. The simultaneity of extremes. After all, that was the way of all things, of life as a whole. The antinomic aspects of existence are things that can only be taken together. So death could be the point in time nearest to love, and wonder inextricably linked to decay and ugliness. Something like catching yourself using the most obscene expressions in bed to say I love you.

I'd heard of orgasmic death on several occasions. That was how the former Cardinal of Paris died, for example, when he was over seventy, in a whore's attic, in the name of the Father, the Son and the Holy Ghost. This was a unique example of episcopal epectasy. Searching through the annals of history, you can also find a presidential epectasy: Félix Faure's mistress knew the secret of fatal fellatio Third-Republic-style. As the saying went, he'd lived like Caesar and died like Pompey, a man sucked dry.

I thought there was a certain beauty in dying from loving life too much. By way of comparison, my grandfather had died taking a pee. That was probably when I first thought how sweet it would be to die in Lou's arms.

4

Trying to live more in the present, I lit a cigarette. Strangely it brought to mind an argument we'd had, perhaps our last argument. I'd told her I didn't like her smoking, I thought it didn't suit her. She lost her temper, it was none of my business, she said. She was quite right. Except that morning I'd read that, according to statistics, one cigarette knocked six minutes off your life. The calculation meant absolutely nothing, it was just meaningless numbers, but it struck me I could see all the years we might have lived together going up in smoke.

I finished my drink and stood up; Charlotte asked if I was going to dance. I started to laugh, don't ask me why, I suppose my clear-headedness was losing ground to the alcohol and I was pretty anxious about Lou not showing up. She gave me a look that I took a while to interpret as an insult in the language of the eyes. Abruptly, I sat down next to her and took her arm to have a little chat; she immediately pulled away. I figured she could bridge the distance between me and Lou and, in my misery, which was on the same scale as my desire, I was perfectly prepared to walk that bridge, ride roughshod over it to get to the other side, the one that fascinated me so much. Charlotte apparently wasn't very keen on me, she glared at me again with her dark eyes. The moment I realised that, I was already standing on the bridge. Hard to backtrack.

After a few general comments, I wanted to move on to talking about Lou. But, without even giving me time to say what I wanted to say, she fired at me:

"You don't know how to love anyone, you're a cold-hearted misogynist."

Her succinct judgement rang in my head. I didn't say a word. Florian, on his way back to join us, came over and sat between us.

"Is it me you're accusing of misogyny? Me, the man who's so fond of women that he gives up his quiet nights for them?"

"No, him."

Florian turned to me, looking amused.

"The reason he's a misogynist is that he believes men and women are different. All we have is facts. For instance, apparently dogs only see in black and white. It doesn't mean we don't like dogs. Alternatively, the only function of cockroaches' brains is to control reflexes. We can't escape the fact that we're just one life form among many, women and roaches alike."

"Oh fine, be like that. I'm serious."

"So what?"

"So he should cut Lou some slack. It would do him good. Anyway, what harm would it do?"

I looked around as if I couldn't care less, then stood up.

5

I wandered about for a while, feeling completely lost. I watched what was going on around me, the way people were moving, the way they were closing in on each other and kissing. I began to realise that Lou wasn't coming.

I'd seen her a month earlier at Charlotte's. Someone had knocked at the door, no one had warned me she was coming and, when the door had opened slightly, I recognised the woman who, for a long time, I'd called the love of my life. That evening she was wearing a sailor T-shirt; blue and white stripes ran round her body, her breasts, her shoulders, like the coloured rails of a train I would have liked to catch again and again, and definitely never miss.

We kissed hello like normal. Then, before we knew it, a load of strangers had intruded on us, the dinner party had turned into a proper party. I'd been so taken aback to see her again that I'd desperately tried to find some signs of imperfection on her body, in what she was saying, in the way she walked, looked around, anything that might have distanced me from her, made her look unattractive or vulgar. But it was no good: carefully examining her body, her figure, the tone of her voice just brought back our past relationship. So much so that I'd decided to leave.

I went into the back bedroom, down the long white corridor that seemed to lead to the end of the world, to get the jacket I'd taken off when I arrived. I couldn't describe how I was feeling. I turned the handle silently and took several steps into the darkness which, as my eyes adjusted, soon became increasingly less dark, revealing glimpses of bodies moving, a thought instantly confirmed by explicit panting. When I realised some guy was fucking two girls on the bed, three metres from where I was standing, I was a few paces from the door and a few paces from where they'd carefully deposited my jacket. Some intuition, probably linked to the survival instinct, made me hold my breath and I stood there, motionless, in the dark with a ringside seat for a show that I really wasn't in the mood for that evening. The guy was lying on his back, one of the girls was sensually sucking him off while the other crouched above him, his face between her thighs. They were obviously trying to be quiet in their pursuits. They hadn't spotted me. I had absolutely no idea what to do and the images unfolding before my eyes weren't conducive to making a snap decision. If I retraced my steps, I had to leave without my jacket, if I kept walking, I gave myself away. I was trapped in what seemed to be an impossible no-win situation. Expressed as a metaphor, I'd say I was in the same position as the explorer who finds himself trapped in his igloo with wolves outside waiting to eat him if he comes out, while, inside, the cold is so cold that his breath is turning to ice on the igloo walls, gradually shrinking his survival space (broadly speaking, whatever he does, he's screwed). Eschewing crappy metaphors, I'd say prosaically I was in deep shit.

I didn't bank on help from Charlotte, who burst into the room just as I'd taken it upon myself to reach out timidly for my jacket, a movement she interpreted as a vulgar I'm-getting-dressed-after-fucking-the-others gesture. She began yelling; it was her bed, to be fair, and she'd just found three or four (depending on the version) people in it. At her yell of alarm, the whole gang came to greet us. What's going on? What's going on? I was about to explain that I was just passing through, when Charlotte ordered us to leave, frowning to contain her anger and disgust, and pointing, under Lou's scornful gaze, in a direction that was probably indicating the front door. A few seconds later, I found myself alone on the second-floor landing, with the three risk-takers from the end of the corridor. You could say I'd messed up our reunion.

I'd called her the next day. I suggested we have dinner at a restaurant. She told me she was tired and she was going to go to bed early, she was very busy at work, her grandmother's dog had died of a heart attack and a whole load of other stuff, but another time maybe. The coldness of her tone froze me to the spot. I spent an entire night wondering why she meant so much to me. We hadn't seen each other for six months and her appearance had been like an electric shock. I called her again the next few days to clarify things, clear my conscience or the air at any rate, but she didn't pick up.

I thought back over it all, over Charlotte's heartfelt advice, and things now seemed brutally clear: Lou wasn't going to turn up tonight. She didn't want us to see each other again. I played dead for a few minutes, stretched out on the burgundy banquette, beset by romantic, suicidal thoughts. I felt as if my life, until then, had just been a succession of failures.

I don't think I'm revealing anything new about human nature when I say that a fundamental duality runs through the whole sphere of desire, that we're constantly caught between two impulses we'd like to act on simultaneously: sex and emotion. The things we say are often imbued with this duality. *Making love* and *fucking* are two very different things, although both can achieve their own quota of eternity. The territory is clearly partitioned: you make love to your wife and you fuck your mistress; you make love to the woman you love and you fuck all the others. There is something about fucking and sex that isn't a million miles away from murder, rape, and the primitive violence of desire. The word often has pejorative, even vulgar, connotations. Like all words marred by uptight moral beliefs. As it is, Judas went down in history with a kiss and so did Joab when he killed Amasa. The couples who stay together for years without lying to each other are probably the ones who let themselves have it both ways: they fuck as well as making love. I'd never fucked Lou; we made do with the tenderness of love and then, one November day, she left.

After she'd gone, I found myself back in a vast emptiness. Then, once the pain had subsided, I told myself it was no longer a bad thing, I was at last able to regain the freedom she'd stolen from me. So I threw myself into a frantic flurry of sham seductions, under such low skies, gravitating towards such ugly voices. I wanted to know as many women as possible, as if to make up for the time I'd been marking with her. As if avenging my own naivety, my own hopes, delusions, my love, my heart, Lou whom I killed a little bit more with each act of penetration.

I'd already been playing dead for a while. The others must have thought I'd drunk too much again, which actually wasn't way off the mark. Then, suddenly, life regained its ascendancy with a vengeance, I felt an overpowering hunger, an urge to devour everything going.

In the end, I went and danced like a man possessed. The decor spun round at dizzying speed. I passed faces and voices that weren't unknown to me; I was convinced I was in another world. People were standing side by side, like stupid automatons. Jennifer was just in front of me, she was even rubbing against me, if I'm not mistaken. She had engineered things so she was showing a great deal of cleavage, ample enough to drive a priest to suicide. Fortunately, I wasn't a priest.

I knew I'd be leaving with a girl that evening, it didn't matter who. It could be Jennifer. Perhaps Carmen, her eyes blue as a far-off sea; luckily, that's exactly where I wanted to run. Perhaps a different girl I didn't know and whom I'd surely never know. It was simply a case of choosing the best anaesthetic. My soul, supposing I still had one, was fractured into thousands of tiny unhealthy desires.

Yes, who cares who it is. We'll fuck, but I won't be totally into it. I'll be there and somewhere else. Our bodies will move one inside the other and a mechanical image will come to mind. Something to do with well-oiled pistons.

At some point, she'll come, she'll cry or something. Then I'll wake up the next morning; it'll take me a while to work out where I am, the room will spin, it'll spin very slowly, before all its components, the window, door and cupboard, settle into their surroundings. I'll see one of my shoes at the foot of the bed, proving that I existed before that moment. I'll be almost delighted by this poetic awakening until I discover the body of a woman I don't know next to me. Then I'll climb out of bed quietly and leave without a trace, like a thief snatching a small piece of the world's absurdity.

7

I saw perfectly well where that evening was leading, into what world, what hell, it would take me. The end appeared together with its beginning after all and we'd fall asleep, afterwards, exhausted by so much poetry.

I belong to the generation of assassins. Of those who, come spring, have forgotten why they should feel emotion.

PART TWO

Chapter One

Put our love in the washing machine.
Alain Souchon

Warning

WE FORGET where we come from so quickly. When I was a boy, the plan was to give me a puppy. I remember that I skipped school to be there when it was born. It happened in my neighbour's kitchen. I'd waited for its birth for several days the way children wait for Christmas and it was the most shocking episode of my life. The bitch was sitting on a tatty green cushion in a wicker basket, eyes wide open, showing no fear, no emotion. I crouched opposite her to see the pups come out, studying her living belly. The woman next door massaged it during the contractions to soothe her pain. Everything was going fine; I was about to see something spectacular at last. Then it happened: she pounced on her pup as soon as it emerged from her bloated womb and tried to eat it. She had a crazed expression at that precise moment, I remember, I was crying with helplessness, it was awful. She sank her teeth into its innocent little muzzle and tried to swallow it as a boa constrictor would have done. The puppy was screaming with terror, an animal's scream. They pulled it out of the dog's crazed throat. It was bleeding all over and seemed on the brink of death. We tended it for days, my next-door neighbour even talked about putting it out of its misery by drowning it, but finally it recovered. They gave it to me. I called it Moses, because it was a survivor. It grew into an incredibly handsome dog. And then, when it was one, they found it run over, three streets from my home.

I still felt beside myself with rage at the unfairness of this, but I'd never have thought that, a few years later, I'd use the same murderous methods as a crazed bitch to kill the love growing inside me before it was too late.

A man forewarned

I'd finally come to a decision when I woke up. I was going to kill Lou.

This decision had been lying dormant for days and nights, but I hadn't managed to take the step intellectually. I knew now she was never coming back to me, that she'd left for distant parts and we were forevermore in different time zones. But, paradoxically, I continued to cling to a faint hope that completely paralysed me. The fact that I knew there was something illusory about my hope didn't detract from it, just as knowing you are dazzled doesn't detract from the love you feel. I even tried to persuade myself that my dazzled sight just showed the proximity of the sun. But there was no sun on the horizon, despite my burning eyes, no sign, and, as they say, light cannot be deduced from darkness.

So, back to killing her. I'd considered various ways of carrying out this plan and, to fire my imagination, I thought back to all the times she made me suffer, all the times she didn't spare me, out of cruelty, out of spite. Her harsh words, the unbearable scorn she sometimes poured on me for no good reason. I thought back to the time she disappeared for seventy-two hours straight without contacting me, to the anxious nights spent imagining her gone for good, then her sudden return, her return without explanation or apology. I thought back to our arguments. All the signs of her infidelity. And particularly to the last day of our relationship, the worst: I'd gone to the Jardins du Luxembourg, to an out-of-the-way spot where we often went, she and I, one of those spots that was ours because we'd found it together. I had two hours to kill between lectures and I'd thought I'd go there to read for a while. I was sitting on a bench; it was November. A few pigeons were fluttering around. It wasn't too cold. Then suddenly I heard a laugh; it sounded like Lou's. There was a couple kissing two benches away and I was just thinking how weird it is that love gives a voice a tone all its own, when I recognised her in the arms of another man, less than twenty metres away. I watched them for a while, in tears, out of sheer masochism and the hands of my watch turned. As did my life, permanently, just as wine turns to vinegar.

Killing her. A host of images came to mind. I took them from my dreams, the reveries of a modern man. I saw myself licking her cunt, I heard her moans, her body tensed. I held her thighs apart, I held them forcefully so she'd know I was there. I was drowning in a sea of secretions, my nose and mouth lost in that obscure zone. Vertigo is a salty fluid; I penetrated her with my tongue and she gave an infuriating, hypocritical little cry. Then, for no reason, I clenched my teeth. I waited a moment. Then I clenched them even harder. I bit her labia until I tasted blood spurting from her wounded flesh. She screamed but I wasn't listening any more. I ripped part of her clitoris off, I ripped her sex apart, I tore it to shreds and I ate it.

This was just an example.

When I was taking my shower, I thought again about the meaning of my surname, Zeller, probably inherited from my father, which, in German, meant both *monk* and *prisoner*. For years, I'd thought it contained a real paradox, then I realised it referred to just one thing, a *cell*, a room that was closed off and isolated from life. In that respect, my name suited me rather well.

I might be a prisoner, but I had an escape plan.

To my mind, the most effective method involved doing what I had been doing for months, just adding an extra element of awareness, since real crimes are premeditated. I had to stop bottling everything up inside, release all those primitive forces, rediscover my prehistory and rip through the superior amnesia with which we're supposed to live. The best crime, the best revenge, was to cheat on her, cheat on her as much as possible, defile her memory with fleeting moments of pleasure.

Light-heartedly getting down to action

I had to take my clothes to the dry-cleaners. I usually went to the one just below my apartment, but I'd decided not to go there this time, because a man called Richard was always there, and I didn't want to see Richard again. I'd seen him a couple of weeks ago, he'd vaguely reminded me of someone or other, an actor or presenter, and I'd stared at him trying to jog my memory. As soon as he turned to look at me, I instantly looked the other way so he wouldn't suspect me of any dubious intentions. However, despite my precautions, it wasn't long before he was imagining all kinds of weird things and started talking to me. I immediately left the dry-cleaners but he followed me. It was so hard to get rid of him that I'd decided not to go back to the dry-cleaners at Saint-Paul. Florian recommended the one in République. According to him, one of the most beautiful girls in Paris worked there. So I had two good reasons for catching the metro. And that was when it happened.

I was waiting on the platform like everybody else, casually looking at the people around me. Several general information messages had already rung out. I'd expected the worst, like they'd temporarily closed the line due to a suicide on the tracks, but every time it was just a warning for people to be on their guard against pickpockets. Everything seemed to be running wonderfully smoothly. And when the metro finally arrived, I'd doubted it was really there. Apparently, thirst can make you suffer from mirages in the desert. Reality is also apparently an illusion due to a prolonged lack of alcohol. I'd noticed that an absence of thirst also had these properties. So I wasn't really sure whether I should trust what my eyes were telling me: the metro simply pulled into the station. But I hadn't seen anything yet. The most unbelievable thing was yet to happen. The machinery of the train squealed, whined and raged, and a door finally stopped just in front of me.

Just in front of me.

No need to make a move, except to step into the carriage like a prince. Had I made my peace with fate? Was the door opening in front of me a sign, an indication that I was now one of the chosen? Nothing pointed to my customary bad luck. There was definitely something odd going on.

Metaphysics of the washing machine

I usually dropped my clothes off at the dry-cleaners on a Tuesday and picked them up on a Thursday. It was one of my habits.

Today was Saturday. I wondered if the dry-cleaners at République would be open on Monday. There was a party at L'Enfer next Monday and I was determined to wear my white suit. Like everybody else, I'd woven a dense web of habits and I struggled to break free from it, a fact that I attributed loosely to the specialised nature of my life. I wasn't very widely travelled, for instance. I'd been born in Paris and sadly everything seemed to point to me dying there. I'd crossed the Atlantic once and had felt like a philosophy lecturer in a nursery school. I'd also been passionate about deserts, but I hadn't taken it very far; like so many other passions, I'd abandoned it along the way, in disillusionment. At the same time, I'd lost my capacity for wonder, an innate childhood capacity whose loss seems to suggest that life is a slow fall, not into the world, but into oneself. I no longer knew how to marvel at nature and this loss took the form of unfounded fears. I'd wondered at least twenty times what I'd do if the dry-cleaners at République wasn't open on Monday and it felt like a huge problem.

Another problem: the more I wore my suit, the beiger the fabric was turning. With each wash, I realised it was losing a little more of its initial white. There had to be a product that would restore its original colour. I was sure of it.

In the metro, a woman carrying her toddler sat down next to me. She looked like a Breton peasant or, at any rate, someone from the provinces; she smelt odd. This certainly wasn't the moment to piss me off. She was tenderly cradling her brat, who wouldn't stop crying. Another, older, woman opposite was watching the scene with staggering compassion. The mother was doing her best, but that scrap of pink flesh continued to yell as it looked me straight in the eye. Nothing got on my nerves more than people's baseless wonder at these tiny individuals. A baby doesn't automatically deserve to be loved just because it's a baby. I'm sorry, but there are just as many stupid babies as there are stupid adults. There are unfaithful dogs, affectionate dogs, intelligent dogs, silly dogs, etc. Same goes for people. Why wouldn't it be the same for babies?

I put my hand on my chest. Through my shirt, I could feel the elongated shape of the Stanley knife I now carried on me. I knew I had the metal that would kill Lou resting against my heart. For a minute, I pictured myself pouncing on the kid and sticking the blade in his eye. The horrific nature of this image even gave me a start.

The old woman opposite smiled at me knowingly and I smiled back, a little absent-mindedly, with a strained twist of the mouth that could, with a little imagination, almost resemble the by-product of a smile. She repeated the tactic with a grandmother's irritating kindness and I suddenly realised she thought I was the ugly brat's father. This mix-up was more than I could bear, so I got up to find a quieter seat further down the carriage.

We arrived at République. I took the exit Florian had suggested and, a few minutes later, I was standing in front of the dry-cleaners. I'd expected it to be shut just for today or something, but no, everything was as it should be. I hadn't even forgotten the bag with my things. Something was definitely wrong.

Inside, an elderly Chinese lady was serving a woman just in front of me. An oriental-sounding bell had rung when I'd pushed open the small door. The smell of detergent hung in the cramped quarters of the dry-cleaners. A young woman came out of an invisible door and walked over to me. This was probably the remarkable girl Florian had told me about. Just at that moment, I thought about a strange link I often made between the moon and the Chinese. I'd read an Indian mystic who claimed that the Chinese came from the moon. This idea had seemed ridiculous until now. But, noting the unaffected way she walked over to me, the idea gained new credence in my mind. This girl had a moon face, she was moon-coloured. The colour of the full moon, to be exact.

She greeted me with a slight nod, before taking my bag, writing out a small slip of paper and pointing to the date when I could come and collect it. She obviously didn't speak French. A button on her blouse was undone, showing a glimpse of the sweeping curve of her demure bust. I thought she was very attractive, although disappointing in the light of what Florian had said. The old lady shouted something to her and she disappeared into the back room. The writing on the slip said I could collect my things from Monday.

Eternal return

I walked back to Bastille from République. It wasn't the nicest area of Paris, but it was still better than the hazards of taking the metro. I thought vaguely about the Chinese girl. I wondered how old she was. From what I could see, she was quite young. I imagined her naked or wearing knickers and this pleasant daydream serenely beguiled the time. Until, suddenly, I realised the mess I'd just landed myself in.

If I ever have to be decapitated, I'd like the blow to be quick and clean, cutting short the pain and my life at one fell swoop. But I sensed a blunt or crooked blow coming.

The type of blow that gashes the flesh, then bounces up and stops, inexplicably. I sensed the lie coming. I sensed the false death, the half-death. The uncertainty.

Had my mobile been stolen or not?

In any case, one thing was certain, it wasn't in my pocket any more. I rummaged around but to no avail: it was nowhere to be found. I stood there for a while rooted to the spot, not knowing how to react. Impossible to picture the last place I used it.

A certain talent for good sense made me reflect that it wasn't the end of the world, after all, it was just a phone. But you could only get the tariff I was on at Christmas. In practical terms, it gave me free evening and weekend calls. Another excellent offer like that wouldn't come along for months. More importantly, I was secretly waiting for a call from Lou and I was almost certain she'd phone me. This was really not the time to lose my bloody mobile.

After the party at the Star, before my murderous res-olutions, I'd decided to make one last-ditch attempt. At first, I'd planned to send her a love letter. Then I changed my mind. There was something ridiculously heavy-handed about that kind of approach, something corny that wouldn't count in my favour. The poet who first compared a woman to a rose was a genius, as the saying goes, the second, a moron; and I certainly didn't want to be taken for a moron. So I sent her a packet of orchid seeds. With a note saying that at first I'd thought of sending her a bouquet of flowers already in bloom, then I'd had the idea of having a cubic metre of soil delivered to her door with these seeds so she could make up her own bouquet, but in the end I'd decided that just the seeds would be enough to say what I had to say. She probably didn't know that orchids, according to the poets, are the flowers of death.

I didn't know why, but I was convinced she was going to call me (in any case, that was the only scenario that could have saved her from certain death), and the sudden disappearance of my mobile only strengthened that conviction.

I had to proceed methodically. There were only two places it could possibly be. The metro and the dry-cleaners. Remembering the warning about pickpockets in the metro at Bastille was enough to throw me into a complete tailspin. I could already see myself on one of the canary-yellow seats on the platform waiting for that sodding train. It was easy to imagine some guy walking past without attracting my attention and stealing my mobile with professional skill. Or when I was on the metro. The woman, her kid and the old lady might have been in league. The child had been there to distract me and the old lady to soften me up, while the woman nicked my phone. The other possibility was the dry-cleaners. I might have left it on the counter. This was the most comforting scenario. But, if that were the case, they could easily claim they hadn't seen it. So, heading back to the Place de la République at a run, I imagined the heated argument I'd probably have to have at the dry-cleaners to get my phone back.

Amen

The door wasn't locked, but a wooden sign said *Closed*. No bell rang when I walked into the small room. There was no one there. It was a moonless night, despite being broad daylight. I tiptoed forward. My phone wasn't on the counter. I walked round it. On the other side was a whole community of bed sheets and slips of paper. I opened a few drawers, without making any noise, glancing regularly at the entrance door, since I guessed the old lady could come back any time. It only took two or three minutes at the most.

Suddenly I saw my phone in one of the drawers. Amen. I could breathe again. It was intact, familiar. I'd simply left it on the counter and the old lady, with good intentions, had popped it into this drawer so she could give it back to me later. Life was good after all. My initial impulse was to listen to my voicemail. You have no new messages. Fine. Tired out by the race from Bastille to République, my body was flooded by a feeling of relief. Everything was back to normal at last. I was just about to leave when I heard a noise in the back room.

May upset young children

It was the sound of a woman. She was humming. My thoughts immediately turned to my Chinese girl. The intimacy of her inaccessible voice made my head reel. I took three steps towards the door keeping us apart. There was the sound of water running on the other side. I pictured her taking a shower.

I stayed there for a while, pressed against the door, a fierce desire growing inside me. I kept glancing at the main door so that I wouldn't be caught out. I checked that I still had my Stanley knife on me. Then I silently pushed open the door.

She was washing something, sheets, in a beige bowl. The room was filled with a thick cloud, steam perhaps. She turned round suddenly, frightened. She said something I didn't understand. The button from before was still undone. A minute went by in silence, because neither of us was sure of our role. I just looked at her body.

There was another noise, the old lady was coming back via the main door, so I went over to my Chinese girl, slipped my hand inside her blouse, bursting another button. She closed her eyes, I slipped my hand inside her blouse as far as her hot little breast, she didn't say anything, I caressed it gently, then I placed my other hand between her legs and, through the thickness of the cloth, I could feel she was aroused, I wanted to touch her body, steal its beauty, in two or three moves; I took her hand and placed it over the bulge in my trousers, I wanted to kiss her, but the old lady was coming, so I ran into another room, I opened the window, which gave onto the street, climbed out and ran away.

Chapter Two

I am a lone monk walking the world with a leaky umbrella.
Mao Zedong

TWO DAYS WENT BY and nothing special happened, apart from my ongoing impression that time was slowing down. No news from Lou. In my dreams, she called me "my angel"; in daily life, she didn't call me. I began a gentle descent into melancholy, but stopped myself, doing what I could to keep my spirits up. The method was simple. It involved not thinking. Instead of sitting down and thinking, I just sat. Thinking is a melancholy activity, and melancholy often shapes our perception of the world, hones our reasons for despair. So whatever you do, don't think.

I had for instance phoned Laure, a girl I'd met at a party two weeks before, whose face was starred with constellations of freckles. She was there with some bloke who worked in TV, and we'd chatted a little at the bar because we didn't know anyone. She was studying architecture. And then, in mid conversation, her bloke had come over to fetch her, looking daggers at me; apparently he wanted to introduce her to someone.

That evening, when I was undressing, I'd found her phone number on a scrap of paper in one of my pockets, which shed new light on what she'd said about hoping to run into me again. On the phone, we chatted again for a while, I even cracked a few jokes and I felt as if I'd liberated myself from Lou, rediscovered my zest for life. I'd thought that the only thing left of her was a faint electrical discharge that couldn't lessen my desire for living. But as soon as I'd hung up, the sadness returned to haunt me. I'd suggested dinner on Sunday to Laure and she'd accepted. You should always aim for the sun; at the worst, you'll end up in the stars, I thought. Her face was constellated with freckles and, thinking about it, *Laure* wasn't a million miles away from *Lou*.

I took her to an Italian restaurant. Or it might have been Greek, I don't remember. All I remember is that it was in my street, a few minutes' walk from my bed. The bed that would soon be Lou's winding sheet. Over dinner, she tried to impress me by telling me tons of boring things about books. She even gave me a masterly lecture about the myth of the original androgyne which, incidentally, was masterly only in boring me rigid. She explained that, according to Aristophanes, no one had realised the power of Eros and that originally there were three sexes, not two: male, female and a third, comprising the two. All men had supposedly been cut in two by Zeus, after a rather nebulous rage, and from that time onwards were on a permanent quest to find their lost half. I was very clear about my opinion on this matter. I'd always felt I was looking for someone very specific until I discovered it was myself. I'd discovered love; it was self-love. She'd smiled and a waiter had placed the bill on the table.

My bed—a mattress on the floor, blue fitted carpet. You could see the sky through a fanlight when you were lying down. I rented this apartment furnished. Which meant that other people had been on that mattress before us, in the same spot, in the same position, looking at an identical sky. You could even imagine that dozens of couples had been there before us. The ghost of all the lovers in the world was pressing down on us, it was a weird feeling. What we were experiencing was totally unimportant. Devoid of meaning. She began to caress me again, with a sickly sweet look. I wasn't in the mood. I didn't want to see her again. There are some situations that can only be settled with violence. I penetrated her the way you rip something open, I kissed her the way you bite something, I took her from behind, the way you turn your face from the mirror.

After that, I slept a lot. Soon it would be Monday and, with Monday, two events I was dreading were looming ominously on the horizon. The first was the party at L'Enfer. Florian had been sent an invitation for two and had asked me to go with him. I'd not been very keen at first, but when he'd announced in a brotherly tone that he thought Lou would also be there, I became more enthusiastic. And a little more anxious. This was my opportunity to put an end to the cruel imprisonment that was keeping me from life. It was the perfect venue—L'Enfer. All I had to do now was set my demons free. I'd been waiting a long time to do that.

At last I was going to see her again. For a few seconds, I was resolute, uncowed by what might happen. But, in broader terms, I was completely at a loss. I had absolutely no idea what would happen. I was continually see-sawing between incompatible extremes. I imagined how I'd break things off with her. And sometimes (the second after, to be precise), I embarked on romantic meanderings that were completely divorced from reality. In my uncertainty, I'd decided to be prudent. First off, I'd carefully dismantled my Stanley knife and turned the blade round to give me an extremely sharp point. Then I'd planned to wear the suit that was at the dry-cleaners. So I had to go back and see my Chinese girl, and nothing could make me feel more uncomfortable.

If someone had told me that the proverb *One must suffer to be beautiful* was originally Chinese, I wouldn't have been at all surprised.

The much-dreaded Monday morning came with bells, a little too early for my liking. It took a superhuman effort to reach out my arm and turn off my alarm whose ringing had become, in my dream, the alarm of a building I'd entered and from which I had to lose no time in escaping; it was such an effort that, to make up for it, I decided to stay in the building for a minute longer. When I opened my eyes the second time, it was gone ten o'clock. I'd slept through my alarm, but who cared. I was getting used to missing the boat. And we often yield to the insistent pestering of habit. I wasn't even annoyed.

I was supposed to be at work at nine o'clock and, as I was already late, the best thing was not to go in at all. Better to fake a sickie than show a lack of motivation. To be perfectly honest, I hated that job, but it was the only means I'd found of studying. That was no excuse, in one way, because I couldn't stand my course any more, but if there's one thing I've learnt in life, it's that you can't always have what you want. I could always have changed lanes, as they say, but the subjects I was taking suited me fine. It wasn't hard to do well, so I had nothing to lose, except time and my will to live. Maybe the solution was to do something I was particularly hopeless at. If I'd started an international career as a classical dancer, for example, I'd have had everything to gain. Especially as I wasn't very supple.

I stayed in bed until midday. I was daydreaming about the evening. I sometimes imagined scenes where I tore Lou's body apart and emptied her corpse of its heavenly beauty. I also imagined conversations in which I was dazzling, everyone was watching me, and Lou had the face of an angel. From childhood, my imaginary life had run parallel to my everyday life. I preferred it to the brutality of the world. As a result, everything I *truly* experienced felt a little tedious, because I'd already *falsely* experienced it. To such an extent that the notions of true and false had lost any intrinsic meaning and I was left stranded halfway between the two—in other words, nowhere.

After the party, we'd leave together. She and I. I'd take her to a magical place and she'd gaze at me, eyes wide with astonishment. During the day, I'd have visited an estate agent's, claiming that my father wanted to buy a huge apartment in Paris and, as he was in New York, he'd given me the task of viewing the places first. A girl in the estate agent's would have given me the keys to a completely refurbished apartment with a view over the Champ-de-Mars, asking me to come back in an hour. I would have had the keys copied without taking time to visit the apartment in question and I'd have gone back to the estate agent's saying I didn't like it. After the party, I'd have taken Lou to that apartment, which was now ours for the night. Inside, there'd be nothing except empty space and a vast white fitted carpet. Like a carpet of snow. We'd be trembling slightly at our sense of doing something wrong, of breaking a taboo. She would have to stifle nervous giggles. Then I'd bring out a bottle of champagne that I'd hidden there before going to the party. We'd drink it by the vast picture window looking out over the sparkling Eiffel Tower. Then we'd make love on the white carpet. She'd say I love you. I'd tell her I want you forever.

The light reconstructs your fragments,
Reconstructs the particles of your skin and your breasts.
The curve of your gaze
Reconstructs the matter of your hands,
You, all of you, whom I would like to possess.

In the early hours of the morning, we'd leave in the sunshine, we'd walk to the Pont des Arts, she'd throw the keys into the Seine, *with a childlike gesture,* and we'd go home together.

Shortly after midday, I was still in bed, like an arse. I got up. Outside, it was pouring. I made myself a strong coffee and finished a box of biscuits lying around in the kitchen. I realised from the little droppings scattered over my dining-room table that the mouse trap hadn't worked again. Afterwards, I tidied my apartment, which I only did on high days and holidays. I even hoovered the living room; I would have liked to do my bedroom as well, but the bag was full. While tidying up, I unearthed a sock I'd been trying to find for ages, a cheque book that had mysteriously slipped under an armchair and an unpaid bill. Then I took a shower. I'd bought some peach shower gel and its fragrance almost reconciled me to the unpleasant experience of having to undress and stand under water on freezing cold mornings. Then, having done all those trivial little things and having run out of excuses, I forced myself to go and collect my suit. This was the start of a big day.

I knew one sentence in Chinese and this was more or less all I thought about between Bastille and République. The sentence was: *Wu-fa wu t'ien*. Pronounce it as written.

According to certain experts, including Edgar Snow, it meant: *I am a lone monk walking the world with a leaky umbrella*. Out of luck, basically. It could be translated in other ways though. According to Simon Leys, for example, homophonically, it meant: *I have no law and no sky*. I liked this version better. I went regularly to mass when I was little. To tell the truth, my vice even extended to becoming a choirboy. But you can't fault me for that, I was young. Then again, what soul is without sin? Anyway, I'm not sure you can really call it a vice—the existence of a God for children might even be believable. When it came to the adult world, though, suspicious uncertainty was all I had. And nothing got on my nerves more than people blithely claiming they were atheists, as if atheism weren't just as dark and impenetrable.

According to some sinologists, the phrase attributed to Mao also meant: *I fear no one under the sky and on the earth; no God or master; I am a free man.* This new translation by Han Suyin clearly demonstrated the difficulty of the Chinese language and, by extension, the tiresome nature of their remarks. In short, I really didn't want to cross swords with my Chinese girl.

The Chinese are far too complicated.

On top of this intellectual problem, there was something else. I'd noticed that Chinese women often had very short legs, which really put me off. So that was the Middle Kingdom in a nutshell. Actually, the same thing applied to fat women: their centre of gravity was not the hips but the lower abdomen which meant, according to a theory developed around the Place de la République, that their frontal lobe was subjected to abnormal pressure, making it impossible for them to formulate a coherent line of thought. I'd almost convinced myself of this when I arrived at the small door surmounted by unlit neon signs.

The cramped room still smelt of detergent. A customer was arguing about a blouse with the old lady. She was pointing to a stubborn stain, she was very cross, it was a present. The old lady seemed to be concentrating and didn't notice me immediately. She'd have to use a product that wouldn't ruin the colour. She was bobbing her head up and down so much that it made me feel seasick. I watched the scene dreading that I would see the back door opening and find myself face to face with my Chinese girl. What would she say to me? Nothing, *in principle*, because she didn't speak French, but what about her expression, what expression would she have in her eyes when she looked at me? Suddenly the old lady recognised me. She automatically pulled out a bag with my clothes, placed them gently on the counter and, looking me straight in the eye, gave me a roguish smile. She made a strange sound in her throat, a sound that predated the invention of language, took my money with one hand, and with the other gave me two slips of paper that she had miraculously taken from a drawer.

"For you. It's very important. Very, very important."

I looked at her to try and work out what she was up to, then I left with my things, in two minds whether I should be relieved or not.

Some distance away, I glanced at the scraps of paper. On the first, Li had written her phone number. Apparently, she wanted us to speak. She didn't say what language. The second was a thicker wrapper, it took me a while to realise there was something inside. The packet opened when I pulled on both ends. It was a sort of biscuit, probably a Chinese biscuit. Without much thought, I put it in my mouth. I had to chew it for a while before I realised that a piece of paper was wedged in my teeth, and that it was actually a fortune cookie, one of those tasteless biscuits containing a message, a type of proverb, handed out in Chinese restaurants, particularly in the United States. For the beauty of it, I swore at the top of my voice, before spitting out the sodden message. And, like a good student, I carefully read the tiny print—*Saintliness must be earned; it is not a gift.*

Fine.

And that was supposed to be important? I threw my fortune in the first rubbish bin I saw while remembering, for information only, that one human being in four is Chinese.

Chapter Three

Saintliness must be earned; it is not a gift.

NOW I HAD MY SUIT.

Having nothing special to do, I decided to take a wander round the area. I walked to Bastille, then crossed the Marais, the ancient stone reddish in the light. I spent some time watching the people around me. My mind was filled with dark thoughts. As soon as I let my guard down, I thought about Lou, I thought about the coming evening; I was a complete slave to this obsession, which was annoying. I felt afraid and my feelings of dejection were proving rather unhealthy. In the little park, near the footbridge, I decked a pigeon loitering around by lobbing sharp stones at its ugly head. Then I jumped up and down on its little body to see what happened: a slice of reality materialised in blood red, dark green and yellow: it was very pretty.

I eventually walked home. It would soon be time. I took another shower and put on my white suit. I wavered for a time that was mathematically close to infinity between several pairs of socks, until the blessed moment when I realised they were identical. Marie had left me several messages; she wanted us to meet up again. But I couldn't think about that; I was so tense my stomach was churning. It reminded me of exams. How many mornings had been ruined by the fear of some trivial test? The people who set them make them essential to convince themselves that they exist as social and human beings. They are petty people who use the only power they've been given, which is immense, and whose pay-off is children's fear. But there was a great deal at stake that day. By the end of the evening, I might have become a murderer.

Apparently, a saint is someone who no longer has an unconscious mind and who, as a result, no longer dreams. At any rate, that's what I read in an article on psychoanalysis. (I'd opened a magazine lying around to pass the time.) There was an interview with a theologian who said we were all being sapped by memories that reached beyond problems of a strictly personal nature, that personal development could enable us to break free of them and that therapeutic methods were therefore not all that different from a process of spiritual development. His rationale left me cold, but his definition of saintliness caught my attention and really gave me cause for concern. Because, after careful thought, I realised I hadn't been remembering my dreams for several days. I would wake to emptiness, a complete blank (at the time, I'd forgotten the dream about the building I'd entered and had been trying to escape). So I was no longer dreaming. The obvious conclusion hit me as violently as a proposal of marriage: I'd become a saint.

I reread the article several times to make sure I'd understood properly and every line seemed to confirm my revelation. Then I downed a few beers to consider the significance of the new make-up of my psychological structure—I'm talking about my saintliness, for anybody finding this hard to follow. First off, I wondered if it would enable me to sleep with more girls but, to my great despair, considering that sheer madness was more interesting from an erotic standpoint, I realised that, no, my saintliness wouldn't exert any influence at that level. I also wondered if it would enable me to win back Lou, who was taking up all the room in what passed as my heart. I dwelt on this unanswerable point. I didn't even know if I had a scrap of a chance of getting her back, but, in my uncertainty, I dared to fight on a little, one eye gorged on hope towards the distant horizon, the other, already defeated, contemplating the tea and cakes our mothers provided.

Chapter Four

Drowning: death by suffocation in some form of liquid.

NINE O'CLOCK in the evening. I went out to buy something to eat after convincing myself I was hungry. I was waiting for a phone call from Florian. We'd agreed he'd call me to arrange where to meet. I pushed open the door of a delicatessen and bought a salad. I didn't want anything sitting too heavy on my stomach. Just in case. I went back up to my apartment to eat it. I noticed I was shaking. I thought to myself that fate was really on the ball. I'd just realised my own saintliness and I was going to see the women I loved again at L'Enfer, clutching a Stanley knife. I also thought back to a period when fate was just the assumed name of the gods. The gods, in this particular instance, were certainly not lacking in irony. Or spite, for that matter. A spite that was indicative first and foremost of our desertion. Naively we believe that we've murdered God, when he was the one who deserted us. We have all been left bereft by a God who doesn't exist, or something like that.

I should've felt comforted by this obvious fact, because it implied that everything was implicitly permissible—even revenge, however horrible—but I didn't feel comforted, because I was less interested in finding an excuse for my life than true forgiveness.

The phone rang. It was Florian, another snag. He had a problem and a strange, unfamiliar voice; he didn't sound like himself at all. He explained that he couldn't go to the party, he had big worries that he'd tell me about. He asked if we could have lunch the day after tomorrow. He added that he was really sorry about the party. The invitations were in his name so I couldn't go without him. He hung up and that was that.

For some obscure reason, I stood there for ages listening to the ringtones on my mobile. Then I put on some music, now I had time to kill. I lay down on the floor, on the blue carpet, and my suit got creased but I didn't give a toss. I listened to the same music over and over for at least an hour. *I'm waiting on an angel, cause I don't want to go alone.* Outside, it was probably already dark. Inside, too. I was sure Lou would be at the party. Listening to the music, I imagined all kinds of beautiful things we'd have experienced together. My heart was a child's heart. You always love with your child's heart and with the rest you deceive others and yourself. *Waiting on an angel to carry me home.* A few tears might even have welled under my eyelids, but it was too dark to see. *Waiting on an angel, cause I don't want to go alone.*

Sadness doesn't recognise the traditional frontiers of matter, it takes possession of everything around it and spreads by means of the nostalgic method of con-tamination; we don't just feel sad in part of ourselves, we're swept away by sadness the way a flood sweeps away daffodil shoots; the liquid invades your whole body and stays put. It's called drowning.

I went to look up drowning in the dictionary but the book fell open at the definition of *nucleus* and everything I read reminded me of Lou. *Nucleus*: central part of an object with a different density to the mass; part of a comet that, with the tail, forms the head; central region of a sunspot; concentration of matter at the centre of a galaxy; central part of the planet Earth; piece resistant to the molten matter placed in a mould to form cavities in cast metal; tiny particles suspended in the atmosphere which, by speeding up the condensation of water vapour, play a vital role in starting precipitations.

It just so happened that heavy rain was forecast that evening.

I think about you at night. I think about you during the day. Dawns, dusks and daybreaks, I think about you in every light.

I fell asleep fully dressed.

The next day was Tuesday.

I began the day doing nothing, starting with not going to work. I took my time getting up. I also felt a little out of sorts because I'd just spent the night dreaming that I was destroying the portrait of someone who was as like me as three peas. It was as if I'd come face to face with another *me* and was trying to liquidate that bastard with my bare fists. So my saintliness had only lasted a few nights. I'd gone over to the other side: I was a lady-killer now.

Chapter Five

One must still have chaos in oneself to give birth to a dancing star.
Friedrich Nietzsche

1

MARIE HAD A SMALL, neat, well-shaved cunt. The moment I penetrated her, existence, from origin to outcome, seemed a shrill aberration, a ridiculous absurdity. I was aware of the precarious intellectual position of that thought and the debatable logic that had me see-sawing agonizingly between it and her cunt, but that's the way it was. I felt as if we'd got ourselves mixed up in a fickle business—life—whose cruelty could be seen in the brutality with which it revealed, after a few painful experiences, that it was going nowhere, that it would ruthlessly abandon us in front of a wall, a wall of silence and tears, a cynical wall surrounded by barbed wire. We kept going over the same ground again and again. We kept going over the same centuries-old ground.

What chance did we have in the face of all this? I remembered a writer who said that we should confront life as if confronting a madman. If someone claimed, despite all opposition, that he was a goldfish, then nobody could prove otherwise by undressing. That would mean embracing madness oneself, given that reality is no longer an important factor within the context of madness. It was the same with the world—we knew we were justified in not taking it seriously because it was so absurd. Joining the world would have meant accepting that it meant nothing. It would have meant undressing in front of a crowd of hurrying passers-by to prove you were really a human being, not a goldfish.

I was inside her; she was moaning. She was getting very wet and there was virtually no friction; we were navigating an abstract dimension. We were fish, she and I. Fish copulating, admittedly, but fish nonetheless.

2

She kissed me for a long time.

In painting, classical subjects were rejected first, then the technique changed completely, new colours were selected, forms were crushed, bruised and battered, and that was when we entered abstraction, still haunted by the certainty that we had to destroy to exist; and in the end that brought us to the famous white painting.

Music and literature followed suit. The need for destruction, which is characteristic of all generations, all individuals, eventually leads to the experiment of the white painting, the point where there's nothing left to destroy, except oneself. That's what we'd come to. We were spiritually bare. White, not with spotless purity, as at the beginning, but with terrifying, cynical emptiness.

3

Beauty isn't what we travel towards. As time passes, beauty wears thin and disappears into the gaps formed by indifference. Beauty is what we blindly leave behind.

Modernity began the day man started painting rotten fruit and decomposing objects. The day man sensed that ugliness contained a kind of energy that might be more real than the overrated harmonies of archaic beauty. We began to revel in everything that stank, we wallowed in the muck like swine. And now we're stuck in it. We call this the aesthetics of ugliness.

4

It was all rather academic. I opened her small bodice to see her breasts. They were shaped like two fawns, twin offspring of a gazelle. They were a little paler than the rest of her body. She placed her hand on my trousers which she unbuttoned with difficulty. She took my cock in her hand and began sucking me off. She was staring at me to heighten the intensity of her caress. Then she concentrated, the way they do in films, and speeded up, moving up and down for a good five minutes. Sometimes, she drew back a little while continuing to jerk me off and licked my stomach, looking provocatively at me. As I didn't want to ejaculate immediately, I raised her to her feet.

She kissed me passionately, we ran through all the unendurable moves of every lover in the world, she put a finger in my mouth, she bit my shoulder, etc. Nothing was really ours. I laid her flat on her back and began licking her cunt. I heard her moans, her body tensed. I held her thighs apart, I held them forcefully so she'd know I was there. I was drowning in a sea of secretions, my nose and mouth lost in that obscure zone. Vertigo is a salty fluid; I penetrated her with my tongue and she gave an infuriating, hypocritical little cry. Then I lay on top of her, her body weighed nothing beneath mine, and I took her. Before, you might have said: *they made love*.

Already we were no longer seeing each other, although our eyes were open. We were both on our separate sides, alone with ourselves, a dark fog between us. She turned over and we continued to fake love for another hour. I discovered a capacity for enjoyment that had nothing to do with pleasure or eroticism. I was entering my own portion of darkness, guided by hatred, boundless hatred, destructive hatred. I was fucking this girl because I wanted to destroy her, crush her, exterminate her. But I also realised she was just a puppet and I was using her to eliminate all women, Lou and all the rest.

5

In music, beauty depends on repetition. In everyday life, repetition leads nowhere. We have the impression we're experiencing intimate, personal things, but the similarity of our lives makes them ugly. We keep going over the same centuries-old ground, we're hilarious but we're certainly not laughing.

It's unbearable to discover that we're repeating what we've done before. Unbearable to feel we're on a ridiculous merry-go-round. With false horses, made of wood, grinning their false unhealthy smiles. And it's not true that falsehood is a moment of truth. The opposite is less false, as it is. Violence is the only way to react against this feeling of being trapped. Every move, a gentle bite on the shoulder, for instance, just confirms our captivity.

True despair doesn't stem from man's mortality, as we are simplistically wont to say, but from his immortality. It's because we're immortal that life is a tale of suffering. We don't despair because we haven't become Caesar, but because our *self* hasn't become him. That immortal *self* that will never commit suicide, that will never excel, that will remain inflexibly the same, continually obliging us to make the same mistakes, suffer the same defeats, ride the same wooden horse.

We'd already fucked five years ago. I was cynically going back to my past to convey in advance what was lying in store for me soon after. In music, beauty depends on repetition. In life, nothing is created, nothing is transformed. Everything is lost.

Chapter Six

In the rear-view mirror of a fleeting moment …
Henri Michaux

LOU, AGAIN. I saw her in the street a few days later. Summer was finishing its shift. I'd been listening to a musician playing Schubert's *Ave Maria*, practically sprawled over his double bass, for at least a quarter-of-an-hour. It was beautiful, like the beginning of the world. There were some merry-go-rounds by the side of the square. A little boy was crying because his mother wouldn't pay for another ride. A man on a bike almost knocked them over, the mother started shouting and, as the bike was already long gone and the kid was still crying, she smacked him.

I'd like to tell you exactly what happened, rather than recall my inner feelings. Just describe, without paying too much attention to the rest. I saw her near the Café de Flore. She walked past without noticing me. I was on the terrace poisoning myself with camomile tea, and she walked past two metres away. It was the second time I'd seen her since we broke up, she was walking through space enveloped in a long black coat and a thick wool scarf. She was as beautiful as Schubert's *Ave Maria*, a sun had fallen asleep in her hair. I knocked over my cup, spilling tea over my trousers, and the saucer fell to the ground and broke—she kept going without turning round.

I stood up and left without paying. Everybody now knows I owe the Café de Flore thirty-six francs. I walked along behind her. I saw to it I wasn't seen. I wasn't sure whether to run over and kiss her, but I wasn't convinced that was the best thing to do. So I stayed back, in the distance. Like a shadow. The shadow of her dog, like Brel said.

I'd loved that body so much, that body I could see in front of me, weaving in and out of the crowd without mixing with *them*. After a six-month absence, I could still map its geography, explore its contours, its subtle arrogances. I'd always believed it was made for mine and there it was, running away from me on the anonymous pavement of some street or other. I would have liked to tell her I love you, but it was too late. We'd never live together. I had the famous Stanley knife in my pocket, now I was holding it in my hand, I was gripping it as tightly as a paralytic holds a cross.

She stopped at a newspaper kiosk to buy a magazine. That was her all over, my Lou. Always buying magazines rather than books. I sensed I was in danger of being swept away by the rush of memories, but I purged them ruthlessly, I didn't want to remember. I unscrupulously gave way to the temptation of oblivion. All that was left was the facts and our two bodies attempting to symbolise them. She took a left, towards the Latin Quarter. We crossed several roads, walking as far as the Seine. We crossed the bridge and arrived at the Louvre at the base of the pyramid. She sat down by the fountain. She seemed to be looking into it. I was a bit further away, hidden behind a stone statue. I was prepared to follow her to the very end. I kept seeing horrible images in my mind's eye. Suddenly some man walked over to her. He blandly asked her the time. She replied in a similar tone, then burst out laughing and threw herself into his arms. They kissed for ages. Bringing her face close to his, she whispered something in his ear. He put his arm round her shoulder and they walked away.

Chapter Seven

I HADN'T MOVED. I wasn't even sad. Devastated but not sad. This relationship was coming to such a banal end, such a mediocre end, that I'd lost any desire for sadness. I'd hoped for such great things in life. I had, I remember, such high hopes. And here I was at what might be the high point of my meaningless life, this is how things were panning out, winding down to such a trite conclusion. At the very least, I would have liked my unhappiness to be heroic, ghastly, to wreak unprecedented havoc. In reality, my role was less gratifying. I was the man weeping over a sad relationship. A downmarket romance. Left comfortless by his formidable destiny. Lukewarm tears.

I re-examined our whole relationship in a bid to break free of it and the more I thought back over it, the more I had the impression that we'd almost done it, we'd missed out on something, and now it was too late, forever too late. All my hopes cynically paraded past. We'd have travelled widely together. We'd have gone to the desert in the Middle East, to Jordan and Israel. We'd have gone to Latin America, the magical lakes of Bolivia. We'd have seen all the continents and we'd have made love everywhere. It sounds lame, but we'd have had children and all that. I know that's laughable. To say what I'm saying at my age. But seeing Lou walking off into the distance, her head on the shoulder of an unknown man who could've been *me*, but wasn't, I felt as if something had just broken. All right, mate, let it go, the similarity of our lives makes them ugly; let it go, they've got the message.

I had to make the decision to go home. I took the bus for a change. When the sun came out, I watched the streets speeding past the dirty window; I passively watched things letting themselves be caught by my moving view. I watched people walking: I found a name for them, a story, then let them go without finding out what made them tick.

The sky hadn't changed since morning and there was nothing about it to inspire hope for any alteration in the unrelieved grey that blanketed it. The colour of the streets when you're cold. The pavement colour of dull days. Of the sky's exhaustion when autumn is in the air.

Suddenly the sun flooded everything, reaching through the bus window to my almost blinded face. I brought my hand up to my face. On the seat opposite, the division between shadow and light was so sharp that they no longer seemed to be two more or less intense variations of the same light, but two distinct areas in space; I was situated at their precarious, provisional frontier, as if I could enter another world, one that was different, tangible, ubiquitous, yet invisible. I sensed that the sunbeam was about to disappear, that the warmth on my face was growing fainter and that I had to hold on to it. Things would soon tumble back into the grey realm.

I closed my eyes and the sun formed two orange butterflies under my eyelids. I heard the beach in Brittany where I spent my summers, as a child, when everything was simple. I heard the din of the dying waves, the cries of children, the drone of the motorboats, the swish of the windsurfers; I made out the smell of salt carried by the horizon, the sand, the sensation of bare feet on hot sand, the afternoon snacks of stewed apple, the wind, the gulls and the endless blue, my life at high tide, all contained in a fleeting sunbeam.

Then I felt the light withdraw and my memories dissolve. I felt the darkness drop back over me and grey regain its cold dominion. When I re-opened my eyes, it was already autumn.

They say love is blind and that the despair of not being loved cuts deeper than the blade of a Stanley knife: so it was a matter of no mean importance that my tears left behind long red streaks.

PART THREE

Chapter One

I N AUTUMN, the leaves fall because they know they'll be reborn one day. You fall from a very big tree when you fall in love. Gradually we lose our colour, we begin to reek of the crisp fragility of leaves, then a slight breeze carries us towards the bowels of the earth, with no promises, no hope; hope is never in season.

I began imagining them together. Creating a romance for them, lovers' games, a tender bond. Inventing places where they might have met, sentences they might have said to each other and when it hurt enough, I fell silent. The phone rang a few times. Marie was trying to get in touch with me, but I didn't pick up. I didn't know what to do about her. To be honest, I didn't even ask myself the question. I was drowning in my own pain. The pain was becoming almost physical, it was a little ball of metal. I was living with it every moment of the day, sometimes forgetting why it was there. It was gradually becoming disembodied from this sad and ordinary love affair.

I didn't leave home for several days, because everything, outside, seemed hostile. A couple of teenagers kissing. The smell of her perfume on someone else. A woman's laughter. Other people's exuberant expressions of happiness. Anyway, it was warmer at home. I spent some time faking death or invoking it. I depicted myself to Death as a bird escaping the body, as flight escaping the bird, then an impulse escaping flight. But Death didn't come. So I began to think about more effective methods than make-believe. First, I imagined myself dead. To see how that felt. It was quite restful. Even so, it was odd to think that my body was destined to become sand; especially as I personally felt no connection with sand.

First off, I'd planned to go and find Lou. The thought had given me a new lease of life for a few days. Find her and be cruel. I'd even taken up position on the terrace of a café facing her apartment and I'd waited, eyes fixed on the door that didn't open, dreaming of a tragic destiny. But I'd finally given up. Still, I kept the Stanley knife, a crappy Stanley knife bought in a supermarket. I'd taken it apart to remove the metal blade and I'd put that to one side. My idea was to use it to die. I wanted it to be awful. I wanted to take that blade and swallow it. I wanted it to rip my insides apart, make me bleed, so that the blood spread through me. One day, in a fit of melancholy, I put it in my mouth with the firm intention of swallowing it. The blade was cold on my tongue. I closed my eyes and repeated to myself: you're going to die, so this is what your last few minutes feel like. I wondered how long it would take the rising blood to fill my windpipe, for me to choke on my own blood. Deep down, I knew very well I was going to spit out that sharp blade, but I kept it in my mouth, maybe just to scare myself. In the stairwell of the apartment building there was a shabby crucifix hanging on the wall. A perfect evocation of morbidity and perverseness, cherishing torment like a lover, turning the self-mutilators, the priests of death and guilt, into role models. Soon after, I spat out the blade.

The phone rang again. Marie probably, but I just sat there and did nothing, like an animal in its death throes, impervious to the call of the outside world. It even gave me a certain pleasure not to reply, to discover that it was so easy to cut myself off from the world, to take the terrifying emptiness that terrified me and throw it back in its face. I realised I was no longer living, that I was just, like so many other people, a *spectator* of my own life. Sitting in an old leather armchair, I stare intently at the small device that is shouting about the existence of the outside world and I look at it with a smug smile, displaying the human being's final and most formidable power—indifference. I don't pick up. Ah! I can distinctly feel this smile, this false smile bearing so many tears and disappointments, on my silent mouth; I'd like to turn this smug, falsely detached smile on the whole world, like a universal rejection, showing my hatred and misery, my hatred of my misery—and the insects will applaud me. One day, someone will have to make this wretched, pointless world spit out its secrets.

I was aware that my grief was answering less and less to the name of Lou. Sometimes I even went several days without thinking about her. I was obsessed by something much deeper; I was only just beginning to grasp it. I could have gone to get my head examined, but I didn't understand all those stupid references to inner balance. People weren't, in my opinion, engines that can be tuned when they aren't running smoothly. There are old bangers you take in to be repaired when the engine is making funny noises. And then, when they're beyond repair, they're scrapped. Are you hurting? Yes? Well, everybody hurts! That's the source of man's dignity.

I even quickly became fond of my pain. It became a protest against life itself, the expression of an inner resistance to something vague. All I saw around me were pointless stratagems. I wondered what made other people tick. There seemed to be no justification for anything. I was starting to see things in a new light, having been totally blind before. I thought about those terrific storms that sometimes rumble in August, about the power they reveal in the rainfall they bring. I thought about the unsettled air that suddenly appears after the rain has stopped. The new smells. That's where I was. I didn't know yet what season I was moving towards, there were still particles suspended in the air, but the sky had cried itself dry. I was standing on the edge of an emptiness. I'm not talking about Lou's absence. I'm talking about something else. A nothingness at the source of things. I felt like an exile. I was homesick for a land deep within. A land towards which I'd unknowingly always been travelling.

All the rest had been nothing more than a crude pretext. A way to ejaculate the nothingness in little spurts.

Sometimes I dived deep into myself, drowning myself in the strange liquid that formed my make-up. Then I would think about the incident of my dog. I sensed a deep well of tears inside me that had never dried. As if I had never stopped crying quietly. And I wondered if Moses' death weren't the secret source.

They'd bought me a cuddly toy dog in an attempt to comfort me, but it hadn't even come close to denting my childish grief. In my dreams, I often saw the puppy being devoured by its mother, I saw again the shower of blood and the bitch's threatening fangs. I'd gone to fetch the little body, three streets from my house; I put it in a green bag and buried it in the garden. I placed several stones on top to mark the spot. I used to go there to gather my thoughts sometimes, when I felt lonely.

Since that episode, I'd considered birth a criminal act. As it was, I'd seen a woman in labour on TV. A camera was placed opposite the dilated vagina, exactly where I'd positioned myself for the puppy's birth. I remember a pornographic landscape. Sometimes, I'd close my eyes and try to edge closer to that original moment. I couldn't make out anything specific and the few impressions I managed to obtain were just intellectual hypotheses; the real emotions had collected in a gap that was inaccessible to me. A few images popped into my mind, but I wasn't sure how authentic they were. I tried to trace my life backwards and kept hitting hazy patches that weren't in any chronological sequence and had broken loose from my history. These attempts obviously took me right back to the beginning of everything.

Mum had several times described what happened when she gave birth. She'd been rushed to the clinic one Friday evening. She'd felt ill and had been brought in a few days before her due date. The squalid, hypocritically white corridors of the clinic were in complete disarray. The full moon coupled with other phenomena meant that there weren't enough staff to handle the extra work that night. They put mum in a small dark room. They parked her there until they had more staff available. There was a young woman with her, an Algerian woman who had worked in that clinic for over ten years. She had panicked because the baby was presenting awkwardly and she was on her own. Mum didn't want an injection and the pain was growing worse. Mum clenched the sheet tightly in her fists, she clenched her teeth, mum was clenching hard. She even started crying and the nurse didn't understand. She left her for a moment, but there was no one free. She shouted down the corridor, but no one responded. So she decided to deliver the baby on her own. Mum was having difficulty breathing, she wasn't pushing, because of the pain, because of the pain violating her. And yet the baby came out. It was a boy. He was covered with blood and he was cold. His happiness was coming to an end.

The nurse handed him to his mother, but she didn't take him. She continued to scream, to suffer, she was paralysed by pain. The nurse realised there was a problem. A complication. Red. There was blood on her stomach, between her thighs, on her legs. A sea of blood. Mum was losing blood. A haemorrhage. Internal. Her lower abdomen was already the dark colour of wine beneath the skin. The nurse didn't know what to do. There are probably countless reasons why she did what she did, but I only remember a vague explanation, the kind that would satisfy a child. It was vital to increase the blood flow from the vagina. The panicked nurse seized a pair of sharp, narrow scissors. First, she secured mum's hands and legs. Then she roughly parted her thighs. She also parted her disused labia. She was now at the *origin of the world*.

She slid the first blade into the orifice. She had mum's genitals in the scissors. I was to one side, wrapped in the innocence of a towel. Mum struggled. And the nurse squeezed violently and made a cut, lacerating the vagina to enlarge the mangled wound. Mum screamed. An animal's scream. The nurse squeezed again, cutting through the flesh the way you cut through fabric. A shower of blood soiled those first few minutes. They sent for an anaesthetist. She didn't come for an hour. I was put in another room. And a week later, when she had regained the senses that had been fogged by agony, we were finally introduced.

After that episode, I think I remember finding it physically difficult to be parted from mum. There was something incredibly comforting about her presence. A living warmth. I followed her everywhere round the house. When she did her singing exercises, I'd stand a few metres away from her. It is perhaps hard to gauge the full extent of the torments I sometimes suffered during her recitals. When she wasn't there in the evening or when she came home late, I'd get up in the middle of the night, I'd walk through the apartment and take refuge in her bedroom, in the bed she would soon slip into. When she was away for hours on end, she'd leave me the scarf she'd been wearing during the day, the scarf that was supposed to protect her voice. She'd put it under my pillow after making a point of spraying it with perfume. The light was switched off, I heard her footsteps growing fainter, the front door shutting and my despair quickly dissolved into a mixture of tears and perfume. I tried to find positions that might help me forget my physical need to be near her, but I didn't succeed.

On Wednesday afternoons, though, she'd take me with her. I didn't have school and she had a weekly appointment with her singing teacher. Mum had a crystalline voice, a superb, soothing voice that perfectly encapsulated all my feelings for her. I didn't really listen to the music issuing from her mouth. I listened to her voice. Before going up to the fourth floor, we'd stop at a bakery at the bottom of the building and she'd buy me a buttery croissant; it was an unbreakable ritual. We'd hurry up to the fourth flour; I'd already begun eating my croissant, my fingers were shiny and I'd be torn between the immense comfort I received from the attention she paid me and the certainty it was about to end. We'd ring the doorbell and a large door would open before us like the announcement of a little death. We had to be apart for the space of an hour.

I can still hazily picture the living room where I had to wait. There was a round table and on it was an object that fascinated me and took precedence over every other object in the room. A crystal pyramid, as big as a tennis ball, that changed colour depending on the direction of the light. I'd play with it, putting greasy little finger marks on the crystal. I'd examine this object, trying to understand the remarkable law governing it. Several rainbows passed through the pyramid. From the difficulty I had in determining this law, I had deduced strangely that I was holding proof that magic existed and, by extension, happiness. All I had to do was hold it in the path of the light and multicoloured butterflies appeared on the wall opposite. These shapes of light reminded me of the white patches that crossed my bedroom walls, at night, every time a car drove past my window. They called to mind all the little everyday details that the mind invests with life, tales and legends, all the meaningless objects that suddenly become a space ship, plane or animal in a makeshift game. This imaginary metamorphosis took place in a very particular world, of which mum's voice was an integral part. That voice made me feel surprisingly calm as if it embodied all the lullabies she sometimes sang to me when I couldn't sleep or when I felt sad. It could automatically quash all my childish worries, the day's disappointments at school. It lifted me out of time and returned me to a wonderfully sweet place that secretly connected us.

Mum would hum tunes in my ear to comfort me. I remember a dreadful argument that had been resolved like that. I'd told her, one day, that I didn't have any school, because I was determined to stay at home. She made me promise I was really telling the truth and I hadn't hesitated: I'd even told her that the whole school was closed for the day. I'd spent part of the morning watching cartoons, comfortably ensconced in the red sofa in the living room, at peace with life, comforted by the thought that she was in the next room. At that time, I had an almost physical repulsion for school and it seemed much more fulfilling for a child to stay at home near his mother, doing stuff that involved and interested him. I couldn't understand the logic behind shutting yourself away to learn pointless rules. I was a habitual offender when it came to not doing my homework in the evening. I pretended to make some of the effort that was expected of me to pacify mum who seemed to set great store by these daily ordeals, but I rarely did anything more than pretend. I sometimes managed to get out of that hell for the occasional blissful day, but for that I had to bend the truth. I was in a state close to happiness at the mere thought that the others were all at school while I was at home enjoying the peace and quiet. It's ridiculous to say that the sun was created for any other reason than to rise in the morning and set in the evening. I thought it was just as ridiculous to say that a child should be created for any other reason than to be near his mother. And, at school, they expected me to achieve results that conflicted with my wish for life.

Mum found out I'd been lying in the middle of the day, after bumping into another child's mother in the street. I was told first by the cleaning lady, who tended to lay it on thick and who claimed mum was very angry. Inwardly I went to pieces. I was unmasked. There was nothing I could do to escape her anger and, worse than her anger, her disappointment. Mum would be back at any minute, she'd come and see me, scold me harshly, with no affection in her eyes, which would upset me. Lies can't stand proof of the truth. I took refuge in my bedroom, thinking that the cartoons wouldn't help my case, and, sitting on my little bed, I began to cry. I was trying, in my distress, to see a possible way out, but there wasn't any. I'd already disappointed her and I wasn't brave enough to face her. I pictured myself leaving the house and walking far, far away. It had been snowing for several days outside. I saw myself setting off in the cold to pay for my crime. I'd live on what I found, like Rémi in *Nobody's Boy*. This idea seemed really feasible. But already I heard the front door.

I took refuge in the toilet which had the advantage of a bolt on the door. Mum came to see me. She told me to come out. I didn't reply, I was petrified, I would have liked to drown in my copious tears. Or be sucked down by the toilet flush. I could tell she was angry from the tone of her voice. On the other side of the door, I thought she must be starting to regret ever giving birth to me. I hadn't lived up to expectations. She insisted that I come out and as I persisted in a tear-stricken silence that kept her from me, she began talking more gently. But I couldn't answer and I was well aware that this silence was my last chance to make it up with her. I waited another moment, then I sensed she was growing impatient and that she'd soon go about her business again. So I opened the bolt with timid fingers and ran into my bedroom to take refuge on my bed among the soft toys that were always a great comfort at difficult times of my life. She joined me. She sat down next to me. I hid my face and I was crying. My body was shaking. She took me in her arms. She didn't say anything. She just held me tight. Very gently. And she began to hum one of my favourite songs. The story of a little girl looking at the stars. I'd laid my head on her shoulder and I was looking out of the window listening to her voice. My body was shaking against hers, I wanted her to warm me. The garden and the neighbouring roofs were under a blanket of snow. Everything was blanketed with white. I wasn't thinking about anything in particular, I was experiencing this moment as a moment of sweetness. As an immense consolation for my sadness, for everything transcending it. As a necessary absolution.

We stayed like that for a long while, without moving, and I closed my eyes, praying that the moment would never end. Mum.

Soon after, the snow melted and the town was covered in thick mud. I've floundered about in that mud for years. Paradise is only found in the past, when everything was simple and sweet. Later, life deteriorates and the caresses dry up. Pitifully we try to recapture past sunshine, but the echoes fade. At most, all that's left is a vague discharge of truth filed away in our memory.

And a trail of gold through the dark sky, a thousand rocketing birds, frightened by the loud report: "BANG! I'm an adult!"

Chapter Two

When you sail down from the sky …

I WALKED IN THE RAIN for a while. I couldn't remember the code for Florian's apartment block. I called him, but there was no answer, so I waited for someone to come out so that I could go in. A blonde woman opened the door for me. She smiled and immediately disappeared. I went up to the third floor. I rang the bell and heard a flurry of activity on the other side of the door. I don't know why, but I had to see Florian. I had the feeling I'd find something I needed in his company.

The door opened and a woman came out. Her expression was hostile, as if I were trying to sell her something she didn't want. I got my breath back and asked if Florian was in. She replied that I must have the wrong address. She'd just moved in but, as far as she knew, the last tenant hadn't been called Florian. I didn't say a word. I just turned on my heels.

I decided to walk as far as the Seine. I wasn't looking for anything special. I kept walking. I was surrounded by colour. I stopped in the middle of the Pont des Arts. I watched the Seine flowing by. At one point, a woman walked up to me. I sensed that she was there before she spoke. I turned round. It was an old woman selling small bunches of daffodils. The rain had stopped. She held one out to me. I gave her a ten franc coin in return and she went away.

That was when I saw him. He was on his own, a few yards away. A long coat came down to his feet. He was looking straight ahead and the wind was blowing in his child's face. He must have been about six. His hair was the colour of gold. He looked like the Little Prince. He seemed to come from another planet. I wondered what planet he might have come from. I couldn't come up with a sensible answer. He was watching the barges sailing under the bridge. His eyes were shining with wonder. I went over to him.

"Hello."

"Hello."

He was still staring at the barges, frowning as if the sun was preventing him from gazing into the distance.

"What are you doing?"

"I'm watching the water."

"Have you ever been on a barge?"

"No, but I know someone who owns one."

"Does he live on it?"

"I dunno."

He had a sweet expression and I couldn't work out what he was doing standing right in front of me.

"Are you waiting for someone?"

"Yes," he said, with a knowing smile.

"Who?"

"I dunno."

"Are you on your own?"

"No."

He showed me the toy he was holding in his right hand and shook it over the water. It was a toy Father Christmas.

"Did you know that Father Christmas was originally green?"

He looked at me, somewhat amused by my stupidity. Rubbish. Everybody knows that Father Christmas is red. Yes, but before. Before what? I don't know, before. He shrugged. Apparently he didn't believe me. How old was he? Six, maybe seven. Do kids still believe in Father Christmas at that age? I didn't really remember. We forget where we come from so quickly.

"Tell me something. Do you believe in Father Christmas?"

"What?"

"Do you believe in Father Christmas?"

He looked away as if he didn't understand what I was saying. He was busy making his toy walk along the guardrail. It was taking huge strides in the air, almost flying, and reverberating, in his little mouth, with a loud engine noise.

"Can your Father Christmas fly?"

"Dunno."

"He hasn't got any wings."

"Yes, he has."

"In any case, it doesn't make any difference because Father Christmas doesn't exist."

His eyes clouded. His little mouth stayed open, but he didn't say anything. He seemed to be hesitating, holding his scrap of rag in the air as if better to convince himself. Poor boy, he was the victim of a collective lie. He was taking his first step into real life. And I felt it was my job, in view of all the disappointments I'd suffered and that had ruined my life, to warn him, warn him about all the pain and suffering in store for him.

"You've been taken for a ride, young man. It's very simple: people have been playing you for a fool all your life. And there's no end in sight. Quite the reverse, it'll just get worse. Don't expect to be happy, because you'll spend your whole life waiting. Poor boy, you didn't ask for it. Life's a big con. We don't choose to be born, we don't choose the way we look, our abilities, everything's imposed on us. And we have to deal with all that just to survive. We have to go to school every morning so that we can achieve the brilliant result of being forgotten a few hours after we die."

He obviously didn't know how to react because he didn't react at all. I thought I ought to give him some more concrete examples. Be more educational.

"In the beginning there was Father Christmas and Father Christmas was green. It was Coca-Cola who decided to make him red, in an advertising campaign. Nobody knows that, everybody probably thinks it's a load of rubbish. But it isn't, sad to say, that's just the way it is. Father Christmas is capitalist filth. All the more so because he's never existed. I know, you don't believe me. You think I'm lying. People who tell the truth are always regarded as liars, sometimes murderers. But that's how you recognise them. You think I'm lying because you've seen Father Christmas; you recognised his red mantle and long white beard one evening in December. You were little and you didn't see through the deception. Grown-ups have to wear disguises so that children can dream. They're well aware that the naked truth is a nightmare. You'll see, it gets worse. People still wear disguises, but it definitely isn't to give you sweet dreams. One day, we have to become adults. People usually say it's a good thing. But, in actual fact, it's the start of a terrifying emptiness. Did you know that matter is largely empty space? When you examine things under a microscope, you see atoms. Well, atoms are composed of a nucleus and a few electrons spinning around in an empty space. To give you an idea of size, the nucleus is like putting a marble in the middle of the Place de la Concorde. That marble is matter. The rest of the square is empty space. That's why we're largely empty space. The older we get, the more atoms we contain. And the more atoms we contain, the more empty space there is inside us. Life is a birth that has to be compensated for.

"And you will compensate for it like everybody else. You'll be satisfied with little things. You'll invent worthless little suns, pale, sad, ludicrous suns to obscure the clouds. You'll talk loudly to drown out the sound of empty space expanding; you'll be going nowhere but you'll do it at a run. And life will pass by swiftly.

"For a taste of greatness, you'll agree to play a part in love's farce, like everybody else; an ugly romance like mine will suffice. It'll put your mind at rest about your emotional state; you'll cry and that will be a good thing, because nothing is sadder than a heart that doesn't race any more. But, deep down, you'll speak about love because you've heard people talking about it, nothing more. Because we don't love anyone, we're alarmingly heartless, we chase after our lost childhood with the mortal remains of that love and years of wrinkles in place of a heart; love is dead and, as for the rest, we cheat. Anyway, that's what we do best now.

"There are around two billion children on Earth, but not all of them are Christians, and Father Christmas has the good sense only to bother with Christians, which reduces his workload and his concerns to around three hundred million children. If we assume that each house has three children, we can estimate that he has one hundred million chimneys to climb during the night. Father Christmas is thought to have thirty-one hours at his disposal during the night (allowing for time differences and his own movements around the Earth). To be more precise, he has one thousand visits to make per second. In other words, White Beard has a thousandth of a second to jump down from his sleigh, sort out the gifts for the house he's about to visit, climb down the chimney without losing his footing, find the Christmas tree, arrange the presents, possibly make a lightning appearance to the gullible children, kiss them so that he leaves them with eyes full of dreams, believing that life will be beautiful, have his beard tugged without growing impatient, make an about-turn, try to clamber up the chimney, fail dismally, go round via the garden without being seen, whistle to bring the reindeer trotting up, take a toilet break, then set off for the next house. All that, in a thousandth of a second. Even on speed, it would be impossible. Father Christmas doesn't exist."

" ... "

I looked at the Little Prince. I could see contempt in his eyes. And I thought to myself that's exactly how the child I once was would have looked at me if our paths had crossed. My hands were still trembling. I waited for him to give me an answer, to react, but he didn't say anything. I wanted to offer to draw a sheep for him, but I didn't know if he liked sheep. Then he shrugged, stuck out his tongue, and ran off into the distance.

I stood there on my own for a while. I would have liked to delete this sorry story. Recapture the sweet pleasures of life before. At one point, I wondered what becomes of the white when the snow has melted, but I didn't come up with an answer.

I hid my face in the yellow of the daffodils; I named them Lou and, *with a childlike gesture,* I threw them over the bridge. I then nostalgically watched the yellow patch disappearing into the distance with the Seine, reappearing at regular intervals and occasionally becoming one with the water. Just as I was about to conclude that the daffodils were floating, they went under a little wave formed in the wake of a barge and, like the end of a bad novel, were never seen again.